STORM ON THE MOUNTAIN

"Oh, no!" Carole heard her father cry.

"What?" She was barely able to make herself heard above the wind and rain.

"We must have gotten disoriented when we got up so fast," he called, his voice now hoarse from yelling. "The trail's over there, right across from where we just were."

Carole's heart skittered with fear. "You mean we're going to have to cross the mountaintop again?"

Her father looked down at her and grinned. "Are you with me, kiddo?" he asked softly.

Carole only nodded. She was afraid that if she spoke out loud he'd know how scared she was.

Colonel Hanson waited until a clap of thunder rolled away, then stepped out from the shelter of the skinny trees. Again they had to bend at the waist and throw themselves into the wind.

They had almost reached the middle of the mountaintop when suddenly the sky lit up as if a million fireworks had all exploded. A crash of thunder like no other boomed across Carole's ears. The earth itself seemed to tremble beneath her feet. The sky went bright, then dark; then she couldn't see anything. Where was her father? He had been there just a moment before. Then the sky lit up again, and she saw his crumpled form.

"Dad!" she screamed.

Other books you will enjoy

CAMY BAKER'S HOW TO BE POPULAR
IN THE SIXTH GRADE by Camy Baker

CAMY BAKER'S LOVE YOU LIKE A SISTER
by Camy Baker

ANNE OF GREEN GABLES by L. M. Montgomery

HORSE CRAZY (The Saddle Club #1) by Bonnie Bryant

AMY, NUMBER SEVEN (Replica #1) by Marilyn Kaye

PURSUING AMY (Replica #2) by Marilyn Kaye

FOUL PLAY (Soccer Stars #1) by Emily Costello

the SADDLE CLUB

LUCKY HORSE

BONNIE BRYANT

A SKYLARK BOOK
NEW YORK • TORONTO • LONDON • SYDNEY • AUCKLAND

Special thanks to Sir "B" Farms
and Laura and Vinny Marino

RL 5, 009–012

LUCKY HORSE
A Bantam Skylark Book / September 1999

ISBN 0-553-48675-6

Published simultaneously in the United States and Canada.

Bantam Books are published by Bantam Books, a division of Random House,
Inc. Its trademark, consisting of the words "Bantam Books" and the por-
trayal of a rooster, is Registered in U.S. Patent and Trademark Office and in
other countries. Marca Registrada. Bantam Books, 1540 Broadway,
New York, New York 10036.

PRINTED IN THE UNITED STATES OF AMERICA
OPM   0 9 8 7 6 5 4 3 2 1

*I would like to express my special thanks
to Sallie Bissell for her
help in the writing of this book.*

LUCKY HORSE

"I'LL HAVE ONE scoop of strawberry with mint syrup, one scoop of pistachio with cherry syrup, and one scoop of fudge brownie with those bright orange sprinkles." Stevie Lake looked up at the waitress and grinned. "We're celebrating today."

"Uh-huh." The Tastee Delight waitress scribbled on her pad and frowned. "Was that fudge brownie with orange sprinkles or pistachio with orange sprinkles?"

"Fudge brownie," Stevie explained. "Cherry syrup on the pistachio."

"Okay." The waitress looked at Stevie in wonder. "Coming up."

Carole Hanson and Lisa Atwood, Stevie's two best

1

friends, watched the waitress walk back to the counter. Then they both leaned over the table.

"What are we celebrating today, Stevie?" Carole whispered. "International Make Yourself Sick with Ice Cream Day?"

"Yeah, Stevie," said Lisa. "I thought this was just a regular day. We're sitting in our usual booth with our usual waitress, who took your usual *un*usual order."

Stevie grinned, then sighed. "I guess we're celebrating the last Saddle Club meeting before you-know-what starts."

Lisa and Carole stared at Stevie. The girls were all members of The Saddle Club, a club they had started some time before when they had first met at Pine Hollow Stables. The only rules of the club were that members had to be crazy about horses and had to help each other out at all times. Since the three spent most of their time together, around horses, and since practical joker Stevie was the main source of most of the troubles that they needed to solve together, obeying the club rules was not a problem. In fact, they enjoyed it.

"That's right," Carole said sadly. "School. I almost forgot. I like school well enough, but it doesn't compare to spending every day at the stable!"

"I know." Lisa nodded. "Now we won't be able to ride morning and afternoon. Or feed or water or groom our horses every time they need it. We'll have to sit at a desk all day instead of in a saddle."

"Please," Stevie groaned. "Don't remind me."

Lisa smiled. "I've gotten to love being with horses so much this summer that I even like cleaning up after them. I never knew Calypso and Doc that well, but after three months of mucking out their stalls, I feel really close to them."

"Gosh, Lisa," Stevie said with a laugh. "Mucking out stalls is getting a little too close to a horse for my taste."

Just then the waitress appeared with their order. She put chocolate shakes in front of Carole and Lisa and a huge multicolored platter of ice cream, sprinkles, and sauce in front of Stevie.

"Enjoy," she said, shaking her head as she went to take an order from the next booth.

"Enjoy?" shrieked Carole, her deep brown eyes growing wide at the sight of Stevie's platter.

"Yeah, Stevie," Lisa said. "This is a new height, or maybe depth, for you."

Stevie shrugged. "I've got to do something to cheer myself up."

"Anyway, like I was saying, I've just gotten to know so many of the horses so much better." Lisa sipped her milk shake. She was the least experienced rider of the three, but she was catching up fast. "I'm not even afraid of being around Danny anymore. Even after we took him to the dance, I still got nervous around him. I was always worried that something might happen to him and I'd get blamed. After all, he is valuable. But he's such a nice horse."

"Too bad you can't say the same for his owner! Anyway, Danny's not the one you should be afraid of," said Carole, giggling. "Veronica is." Veronica diAngelo was Danny's owner, and also the richest, snootiest girl at Pine Hollow. She'd gotten The Saddle Club into trouble more than once.

"I feel sorry for Danny." Stevie swirled a bite of pistachio ice cream around in cherry sauce. "Veronica loves the way Danny can make her look good at a horse show, but she doesn't really appreciate him as a horse."

"You know he hasn't been ridden in over a week?" Lisa said. "Veronica's been too busy shopping in Washington for her fall wardrobe."

Carole frowned. "I thought Red O'Malley was supposed to be riding him."

"Veronica's furious with Red. She accused him of getting a scratch on her new French saddle and told him not to go near Danny again," Lisa reported. "Now, because Danny's been neglected, he's got some kind of problem with his right front leg. He's got a bandage on it and can't be ridden for at least another week. I saw him in the back paddock. Red's longeing him every day."

"Poor horse." Carole shook her head. "He must

4

have been foaled under an unlucky star to get an owner like Veronica."

"Danny's about as unlucky as our horses are lucky," Stevie mumbled through a mouthful of strawberry ice cream.

"What did you say?" Carole asked.

"I said our horses are lucky. We treat them like royalty. We groom them and water them and love them and ride them almost every day. And now Lisa even loves to muck out their stalls! I mean, how much luckier can three horses get?"

"I guess you're right, Stevie," Carole laughed. "Although I hadn't quite thought of it that way."

Carole and Lisa finished their shakes while Stevie worked on her ice cream. "I've been thinking," Stevie said as she started on her last scoop, the fudge brownie covered in orange sprinkles.

"Uh-oh," said Carole. "When you start thinking, I get worried."

"No, really." Stevie swallowed one orange-and-black spoonful in a single gulp. "Since Friday starts our final weekend of freedom, why don't we spend the whole time at Pine Hollow? We can go over there early Friday morning and not go home till late Monday afternoon."

"You mean spend three nights there?" Lisa asked excitedly.

"Sure. We could bring food and sodas and our sleeping bags and camp out in the hayloft right above our horses. It would be neat. Like one big sleepover with Belle, Starlight, and Prancer."

Carole frowned. "Do you think Max would let us?"

"I bet he would if we asked him nicely." Stevie stopped eating for a moment and brushed one tousled, honey-colored lock off her forehead. "I mean, we'd probably have to volunteer to do some extra chores around the barn, but who cares? We love doing those things anyway. It wouldn't be like work at all."

"That sounds like fun." Lisa's blue eyes grew dreamy. "Living above a horse is about as close to one as you can get."

"Okay," Carole agreed. "Let's meet at Pine Hollow tomorrow and try to convince Max."

"Good idea," said Stevie, scraping up her last bite of ice cream. "How can he possibly turn us down if all three of us wonderful, beautiful young riders are there begging him?"

"I can't imagine, Stevie," Carole laughed as they scooted out of the booth and walked over to the cash register. "How could he say no to anyone who can eat fudge brownie ice cream sprinkled with orange dots?"

The girls paid their bill, then agreed to meet at the stable at ten the next morning. Carole waved as Stevie and Lisa began to walk toward their homes; then she turned and hurried to the bus stop in front of the shopping center. She and her dad, who was a colonel in the Marine Corps, lived farther away from Pine Hollow than her friends, and Carole often had to take a bus ride before she could take a horseback ride.

The bus soon came, and after a twenty-minute jaunt across the little town of Willow Creek, Carole stood at her front door.

I'd better hurry, she thought, turning her key in the lock. *It's my turn to start dinner, and Dad will be home soon.* She pushed open the door. The house seemed emptier than it ever had before. Since Carole's mother had died some time ago, her father had always done his best to be home when she got back from the stable. Lately, though, he'd been busy with a new satellite communications project for the Marines, and the job had required extra hours at work. Carole knew it was necessary, but she still missed hearing him clattering around in the kitchen when she returned home.

"Oh, well," she said to herself as she took off her boots and padded sock-footed into the kitchen. "Thank goodness these special projects don't last forever."

She opened the refrigerator and looked inside, wondering what they could have for dinner. There was some leftover pot roast, some uncooked hamburger, plus a big bowl of macaroni and cheese.

Maybe I'll reheat the roast, Carole thought. *And then*

cook some extra vegetables to go along with it. She put the meat in the oven to heat, then looked in the crisper to see what vegetables they had. Broccoli, lettuce, and carrots. She pulled out the carrots. They were exactly the same color as the sprinkles Stevie had just eaten on her ice cream.

"At least they'll be better for us." She laughed aloud as she closed the refrigerator door. She had just begun to peel the carrots over the sink when she heard a car pull into their driveway. Her father, Colonel Mitch Hanson, was home.

"Hi, sugar," he called, grinning as he peeked into the kitchen. "Sorry I'm late."

"Hi, Dad. How are you?" Carole smiled back at him over her shoulder.

"Other than being late, I'm great. How are you?" He threw a Marine Corps duffel bag on one kitchen chair and strode over to the sink, planting a kiss on the top of her head.

"Fine. Just peeling some carrots for dinner."

"How about if I help?" He opened a drawer and pulled out another vegetable peeler, then stood beside Carole at the sink. "In fact, how about we make a deal? If I help you peel all these carrots, then will you promise not to cook them?"

"Not cook them?" Carole looked up at her dad.

"Right." He held up one carrot. "I mean, wouldn't it be a shame to put this little defenseless carrot into a big pot of boiling water?" He put the carrot close to his ear. "I can even hear it calling—'Please don't cook me, Carole.'"

"Okay, Dad," Carole laughed. "I get the point. You prefer carrots raw."

"Absolutely." Colonel Hanson grinned and took a bite of crunchy carrot. "I mean, why try to improve upon perfection?"

"Okay. I guess that means we'll have pot roast and macaroni and cheese and raw carrots tonight."

"Sounds great to me." Colonel Hanson took another bite of carrot. "Hey, guess what?"

"What?"

"You know how much I've had to work these last few weeks, ever since the Link Life project started? Coming home late and going in to work early?"

Carole nodded. She knew how much she'd missed spending time with her father and how much he'd hated to be away.

"Well, Link Life is almost finished. As of sixteen hundred hours tomorrow, your old dad will be back."

"That's wonderful, Dad!" Carole turned to her father and gave him a hug. "I've really missed having you here when I get back from the stable."

"And guess what else?"

Carole blinked. It seemed like her dad was getting as bad as Stevie in the "guess what" department. "What?"

9

"General Williams was so pleased with all we've accomplished that he gave me a four-day weekend off, beginning Friday."

"Super!" Carole hugged her father harder.

"And guess what else else?"

Carole couldn't help laughing. "What now, Dad?"

"I've arranged for just the two of us to go up to one of the national wilderness areas in the Blue Ridge Mountains. My old buddy Colonel Cheatham is going to lend us his tent and all his new solar camping equipment."

Carole frowned. "His solar camping equipment?"

"Yeah. It's great. We won't have to stay in any cabins or motels. We can rough it just like the pioneers, but we'll be comfortable and we'll be in one of America's most beautiful forests. Doesn't that sound great?"

Carole looked up at her father. A wide grin was spreading across his face. "Gosh, Dad, you know I love to camp."

"*And* I like spending time with my favorite daughter," he said, squeezing her shoulders. "And what better place to do it than out in nature, surrounded by the latest in camping equipment?"

She smiled. "I hadn't thought of it that way, but I guess you're right."

"I knew you'd be excited. Let me go change out of this uniform, and then I'll help you finish dinner."

Carole turned back to the sink as her father hurried

out of the kitchen. She picked up another carrot and began peeling it, then sighed. Why did all the fun things in life always seem to happen at the same time? When she'd started supper she'd been thrilled about the prospect of spending the weekend with Stevie and Lisa at Pine Hollow. Now her dad had come home and told her that he'd planned a wonderful father-daughter camping trip.

She shrugged. It would be great to spend all weekend at Pine Hollow, but it would also be great to hike through the Virginia mountains with her dad. It seemed like they hadn't really talked in forever.

No, when she thought about it, the decision wasn't a hard one at all. Maybe she could sleep over at the stable some other time with Stevie and Lisa. Opportunities to camp with her father didn't come along every day, and she just couldn't pass this one up.

2

"MAX, WE'VE GOT an offer you can't refuse!" Stevie's voice echoed down the corridors of Pine Hollow.

Carole hurried through the sweet-smelling barn, a half-eaten bagel in one hand. She'd overslept that morning, and though her father had been kind enough to give her a ride, she was still late. Stuffing the last bite of the bagel in her mouth, she started to run. She turned the final corner on one leg and skidded into Max Regnery's office. Max, who owned Pine Hollow along with his mother, Mrs. Reg, was sitting behind his big desk just as Stevie was getting wound up to make her final pitch.

"Ah," said Max, smiling at Carole's appearance. "The third and final member of The Saddle Club. I guess this makes it official."

Stevie and Lisa turned and looked at Carole.

"Right." Carole swallowed her bagel and grinned sheepishly. "Sorry I'm late."

"Don't worry." Max leaned back in his chair and folded his arms across his chest. "I'm sure we haven't even come close to the good parts yet."

Stevie cleared her throat and began. "Max, what we want to propose is this: Since we've spent most of our time this summer here at the stable, and since we've learned how to do all the chores so much better than we ever did before, and since now all the horses practically regard us as . . . as blood sisters, we were wondering if we could spend our entire last weekend of freedom here at Pine Hollow."

"Your last weekend of freedom?" Max frowned. "You're not going to jail, are you?"

"No, we're going back to school Wednesday," Stevie explained. "We'd never do anything that would land us in jail."

"But it might as well be jail," Lisa said.

"Yeah, Max." Stevie took over again. "It might as well be jail. We have to sit still for hours at a time and we have to eat this terrible food in the cafeteria and all these dorky teachers make us do stuff like algebra problems and science projects. In fact, it's worse than jail. It's torture."

"Oh, the horror," Max replied softly. He didn't crack a smile, but his blue eyes were twinkling. He

13

looked at Stevie. "And you want to postpone this prearranged torture somehow?"

Stevie shook her head. "We can't postpone it. But we want to squeeze every little drop of fun out of our last days of summer vacation. And if you'll let us stay here for the weekend, we can."

"But we'd work," added Lisa. "We wouldn't just stay up in the hayloft and goof off."

"Oh?" Max's mouth curled up with interest.

"Absolutely," said Stevie. "Lisa would muck out all the stalls every day and I could help Red tack up the horses for the riding lessons and Carole could paint some of the jumps and of course all the horses would be fed and watered and groomed twice a day. And, and . . ." Stevie desperately looked around Max's office. "And we'll sweep out your office and we could even try to shovel up that big pile of manure . . ."

Max held up one hand. "Wait a minute. Let me get this straight. In exchange for bunking down in the hayloft for three nights, you'd be willing to do all those chores?"

"Oh, yes!" cried Lisa and Stevie together.

"Well, I'll tell you something. Mom, Deborah, and I were just trying to figure out who we could get to watch the stable if we took a weekend trip up to Dorothy DeSoto's training farm on Long Island. We'd almost given up on the idea, but if you three are willing to do all that, then this is a deal I can hardly pass up."

"Oh, Max!" Stevie cried.

"But you won't have to start moving the manure pile. I've hired some guys with backhoes to come and do that next week. Everything else, though, is perfectly acceptable."

Lisa and Stevie grabbed Carole and began to jump up and down.

"Wait, you guys," Carole said as her friends bounced in the air beside her. "I've got some bad news."

"Oh no," said Lisa. "Won't your father let you come? My mother let me, and she never lets me do anything unless it's approved by every adult within a ten-mile radius."

"No, it's not that. My dad's big project at work has just ended and he got a four-day weekend as a reward. He's planned this father-daughter camping trip for the two of us." She smiled regretfully at her friends. "As much as I'd love to be with you guys, I don't often get a chance to spend time like this with my dad."

"That's okay, Carole," Stevie said. "We understand." She turned to Max. "Is it still okay if it's just Lisa and me?"

"You don't think just the two of you will get spooked here in the middle of the night? Stables are full of scary noises at two in the morning."

"Of course not, Max," Stevie assured him. "That's kid stuff."

15

Max smiled. "Okay, then. It's fine with me. Just to prove how good a sport I am, you don't have to paint all the jumps. But everything else on your list remains."

"Great," said Stevie, extending her hand. "It's a deal."

As Max shook hands with Stevie and Lisa, his phone rang. With a wave he shooed them out of his office and turned to talk to the caller about dressage lessons.

"Oh, wow," said Stevie as the three girls walked toward their horses' stalls. "I can't believe we're going to do this. A weekend sleepover at Pine Hollow!"

"I'm just sorry you won't be here, Carole," Lisa said.

"Right," grumbled Stevie. "It'll be fun, but it won't be perfect."

Carole sighed. "I know. I really wanted to come, but I haven't had a chance to be with my dad in a long time, and he's so excited about this trip." She looked at her friends. "He's borrowed some really fancy camping equipment that's all run by solar energy."

"Wow," said Stevie. "That's really state-of-the-art stuff. I've seen my brother Chad drool over that kind of gear in his camping magazines."

"I can't wait to see how it all works." Carole giggled. "I think Dad's almost as excited about taking all

16

this equipment up into the wilderness as he is about taking me."

"It'll be a great trip for both of you, though," said Lisa.

"I know." Carole smiled. "I'll just miss you guys a lot."

"Here are some other guys who've been missing us a lot," Stevie said as they turned the corner. All along both sides of the passageway, the horses poked their heads out from their stalls. Their ears stood erect, and their eyes sparkled. Starlight's and Belle's stalls were together, and Prancer's was a little farther down the aisle.

"Looks like some friends of ours want to go for a ride," Carole laughed as Starlight nickered at her.

"Me too," said Stevie. "It seems like years since we've been on a horse."

"Stevie, we rode yesterday," Lisa reminded her.

"I know." Stevie frowned. "I just keep thinking about school and how much time that's going to take away from riding."

"My mother would say you need to get your priorities in order," Lisa said with a laugh.

"Oh, they'll be in order by Wednesday. Right now, I just want to have fun. Last one tacked up's a rotten egg!"

The girls raced to the tack room and got their

equipment. In a few minutes all three riders stood at the entrance to Pine Hollow with their horses brushed and their saddles tight, ready to mount up.

"Whew," Stevie said as she pulled Belle up last. "I think that was a record!"

"I do, too," agreed Lisa. "It's one of the few times you've had to be the rotten egg."

"It's just my school-a-phobia kicking in," said Stevie as she touched the good-luck horseshoe tacked to the wall and hopped up on Belle's back. "And the only cure is a nice long ride in the country."

One of Pine Hollow's traditions was that riders all touched the good-luck horseshoe before riding. So far, no one who had done that had ever been seriously injured.

Carole and Lisa each buckled on their helmets and touched the horseshoe, then mounted up and followed Stevie.

Stevie began leading them to the back of the stable property, where all the trails began. On their way they saw Danny out in the paddock, grazing uninterestedly, his right foreleg wrapped in a red bandage. When The Saddle Club rode by, the big gray gelding pricked his ears and whinnied as if he wished he could come along, too.

"Look at Danny," Carole said as they trotted past. "He looks so sad. I feel sorry for him."

"Me too," said Lisa. "He's such a beautiful horse."

18

"I said it before: He's unlucky," Stevie called over her shoulder. "He's got creepy old Veronica for an owner."

"Hey, could you guys add one more thing to your list of chores this weekend?" Carole gave Starlight a pat on his neck.

"Anything," Stevie said. "Now that we don't have to shovel that big pile of manure."

"Could you take care of Starlight for me?"

"Sure," answered Lisa. "We'll take extra-special care of him, just for you."

"Thanks." Carole smiled. She knew she could depend on her friends.

As they reached the end of the paddock, Stevie and Belle picked up a trot and headed toward the creek trail. The day was tailor-made for a horseback ride. Puffy white clouds floated through a deep blue sky, and late-summer cicadas rasped in the underbrush along the creek.

"Anybody want to canter to our favorite spot?" Stevie asked, grinning over her shoulder.

"Absolutely!" said Carole, and Lisa nodded.

Stevie only had to touch Belle with her right heel and the pretty bay mare moved into an easy canter. Starlight followed, and Prancer stretched her long legs out as well. Soon all three girls were flying along the wide trail in the deep green forest, the warm wind blowing in their faces. They cantered, trotted, and

19

walked until they reached a wide spot by the creek where the horses could graze and the girls could dip their toes in the water.

"Wow." Lisa slid off Prancer. "That was great."

"It was even better than yesterday," Carole said as she led Starlight over to a patch of tender clover. "Starlight just gets stronger and stronger."

"So do we," added Stevie. "I bet we're all much better riders than we were at the beginning of the summer." She sighed. "Now it will all go to waste, though, because of dumb old school. Our skills and muscles will atrophy—that's a vocabulary word from last year—from lack of use."

"Oh, Stevie, quit thinking about it," Lisa said. "School isn't that bad, and you can't do anything about it anyway."

"I suppose," replied Stevie, plopping down beside the creek and removing her boots.

The girls wiggled their toes in the water until the sun grew hot in the sky. Carole and Lisa wondered what their new classes would be like, and finally even Stevie admitted that she was a little curious about who her math teacher was going to be. Too soon it was time to go, so they put their boots back on and pulled their horses away from their happy munching.

They knew better than to race back to the barn, so they took the rest of the trail at an easy trot and the last quarter mile at a walk. When the Pine Hollow paddocks came into view, Carole stood up in her saddle.

"Look," she called. "Danny's in practically the same spot we left him in. Isn't Red supposed to be longeing him?"

Lisa nodded. "He is, but maybe he got busy with a class or a delivery of hay."

Carole frowned as they rode closer to the paddock. As much as she disliked Veronica, she liked Danny a lot, and the idea of a talented, intelligent animal being ignored made her uncomfortable. She wondered if Stevie and Lisa wouldn't start on their promise to her just a little early.

"Hey, you guys," she said, pulling Starlight to a halt right beside Danny's paddock. "Since the longe line's right here and Red seems to be busy, if you two will take care of Starlight now, I'll go ahead and longe Danny. He didn't do anything to deserve this."

"Go ahead." Lisa took Starlight's reins. "We'll look after Starlight for you."

"Thanks." Carole smiled as she grabbed the longe line and crawled through the fence.

The big gray nickered, then trotted up to Carole. She noticed he favored his right leg just a little bit.

"Hey, boy," she said softly as she clipped the line on his halter. "Looks like you're doing okay. We're going to do a little work now—just what the doctor ordered."

21

She led Danny to the center of the ring and walked him in a circle, letting the longe out slowly. As the circle grew larger, Danny's pace grew faster. Carole knew from her work with the vet, Judy Barker, that it was important to keep a horse moving while he was on the mend or his muscle tone would suffer. She worked Danny for fifteen minutes clockwise, then another fifteen minutes counterclockwise. At the end of the half hour, he was warm but not sweaty, and he looked pleased when they stopped, as if he knew he'd done something that would help him heal.

"Good boy," she said, rubbing him between his eyes. She unsnapped the longe line and dug in her pocket for one of the carrots her father had forgotten to eat the night before. She'd planned on giving them to Starlight, but Danny had worked so hard, he deserved at least one. "Stevie and Lisa will take good care of you this weekend," she promised him as she coiled up the longe line and walked to the stable.

By the time she got to Starlight's stall, Lisa and Stevie were just finishing up.

"Starlight's all tucked away," Stevie reported. "He's got fresh water and hay, and Lisa gave him a nice brushing."

"Thanks, you guys," Carole said as she gave Starlight a farewell scratch behind his ears. "You be a good boy, Starlight. Mind Stevie and Lisa—do exactly as they say. I'll see you Monday."

Starlight twitched his nose at Carole for a moment, then turned his attention to his new hay.

"That must be horse for *okay*," Lisa said with a laugh.

"I guess that's it for me," Carole said. The girls began walking toward the stable entrance. "I've got to go home and do a few chores before we leave tomorrow. How about you guys?"

"We need to figure out what we're going to bring tomorrow night," said Stevie. "I've never camped for a whole weekend with twenty-five horses before."

They walked to the end of Pine Hollow's long drive, then joined in a three-way hug.

"I hope you have a great time with your dad, Carole," Lisa said. "We'll miss you."

"Thanks." Carole smiled. "I'll miss you guys, too. I'll think of you when I'm out in the woods, cooking brownies in my solar-powered oven."

"Have a great time," added Stevie. "And don't worry about Starlight. He'll be number one on our list."

"Thanks," Carole called as she hurried to the bus stop. "I know you guys'll have fun. I can't wait to hear all about it."

"Call us as soon as you get back."

"Right," Carole said with a bright farewell wave. "I'm sure we'll have a lot to talk about!"

3

"HEY, CAROLE! CAN you lend me a hand for a second?" Colonel Hanson's voice boomed from the kitchen.

"Sure." Carole opened her bedroom door. "I'll be right there." She tossed a pair of clean socks on her bed and hurried through the house. Her father stood at the kitchen door, his eyes shining with excitement.

"I want you to see all this neat stuff we're taking with us," he said.

Carole followed him out into the driveway and gasped. Tents and sleeping bags and backpacks spilled from the back of their station wagon like a Thanksgiving cornucopia. Carole blinked. All this was supposed to be for a four-day trip to a national park in Virginia. The only place she'd ever seen this much equipment was when she saw her father's battalion going on maneuvers.

"Gosh, Dad," she breathed. "Your buddy Colonel Cheatham must really love to camp."

"He does. Last year he went up to Mount Rainier in Washington State. Almost made it to the top, too." Colonel Hanson smiled at Carole. "Come, let me show you some of these things."

She walked over to where her father stood. Two down sleeping bags were rolled up on the ground, along with a couple of blow-up mattresses. A telescope stood next to two camping chairs, which sat next to two camping armchairs, and two camping stools rested nearby. A special bag for water hung from the door of the station wagon, just touching the top of a thing that looked like a miniature blackboard.

"What's that?" Carole pointed to the blackboard-looking thing. "We're not going to practice for school, are we?"

"Oh, no." Her father laughed. "That's a solar energy collector. You point that black panel toward the sun and it charges a battery inside."

Carole frowned. She couldn't imagine Colonel Cheatham climbing Mount Rainier with a solar energy collector strapped to his back. "And then what does it do?"

"Well, after it charges up, it can run all this other equipment."

25

"What other equipment?"

Colonel Hanson grinned and held up a big lantern. "This solar-powered light bank so that we can read in our tent at night." He turned around, searched through the rest of the equipment, and finally held up a thing with spindly metallic legs that looked like a space satellite. "And this, which is a solar-powered stove, where we'll cook things that we've kept in our"—he pointed at a shiny aluminum box and grinned—"refrigerator." He put the stove down and knelt in front of the refrigerator. "It runs on batteries, but they can be recharged by—"

"Solar power?" Carole finished his sentence for him.

"Right!" He looked up at her. "Isn't this great?" He leaned over and opened the refrigerator. "And look what we've got to eat—spaghetti and fried chicken and brownies. How's that for roughing it with your old man?"

"Great," Carole said, hoping she sounded more enthusiastic than she felt. Her favorite camp food was a simple hot dog sizzled over an open fire. It looked like her dad was trying to see how many gourmet meals he could cook with solar power.

"And," Colonel Hanson continued, "we've got collapsible bowls for mixing up the pancakes, collapsible cups, and a collapsible clothes-drying rack, in case either of us falls into the creek."

Carole blinked in amazement. "What are all those shoes over there?"

"The tall boots are hiking boots. The shorter ones are walking boots. The soft-soled shoes are for sitting around camp, and the things that look like slippers are for keeping your feet warm when you don't want to wear boots at all." Colonel Hanson reached into the back of the station wagon. "And look at these." He pulled out a pair of khaki trousers. "These look like pants, right?"

Carole nodded.

"Well, with just a few quick zips of this Velcro . . ." Colonel Hanson fidgeted with the pants for a moment, then pulled one leg off. "Ta-da! You've now got shorts!"

Carole didn't know what to say.

"And I bet you thought this was a jacket, right?" He held up a tan-colored jacket.

Again Carole could only nod.

"It is. But it's also a vest." Colonel Hanson unfastened the arms of the jacket just as he had the legs of the pants and pulled off one sleeve. "If you're out hiking in a jacket and pants and you get hot, with just four quick zips of Velcro, you can be in shorts and a vest!"

Carole stood there, looking at her father holding up a vest that had once been a jacket, and pants that could soon be shorts, and started to laugh. She couldn't help it. He looked just like someone you'd see on television, selling camping gear in a commercial.

"Oh, Dad," she laughed. "I've never seen as much Velcro and solar energy in my life. Compared to all this stuff you've got, staying at the Ritz would be roughing it!"

Colonel Hanson's eyebrows drew together in a frown. "You think so?"

"Well, it is a lot of fancy equipment," Carole said gently.

"Yes, but it's all so neat and makes camping so much easier. I can remember camping on maneuvers when the only shelter we had was the foxhole we dug ourselves and the only food was whatever we could scoop out of a can of K-rations." Colonel Hanson shuddered. "Believe me, that was not fun."

"You're right, Dad," Carole said. "I forgot how much you've camped on duty." She looked at him and smiled. "But don't you think portable electric blanket liners for the down sleeping bags are a little much? After all, this is Virginia, and last night the low was only sixty."

Colonel Hanson looked at the array of equipment spilling from the car and smiled. "I suppose you've got a point." He reached in and took the two fleecy liners out. But let's take everything else. You never know what kind of weather you might run into."

"Okay, Dad." Carole smiled.

"Have you finished packing?" he asked.

"Not quite."

"Why don't you go finish up, and I'll stow our gear in the car and we can plan on leaving in about half an hour."

"Okay."

Carole hurried back to her bedroom, her head spinning. With all the gear her dad was packing, she wondered if there would be enough room in the car for the small backpack she had planned to take.

Well, if worst comes to worst, she thought with a chuckle, *I guess I can sit with it on my lap.*

She went over to her bed and looked at the things she had spread out to pack. Since they were only going to be gone three nights, she'd laid out three pairs of clean underwear and socks, a couple of T-shirts, a sweatshirt, plus an extra pair of shorts for the daytime and jeans for cool nights. To that she'd added bug spray, a comb, toothbrush and toothpaste, a flashlight, and a new book about horses that she'd bought the week before. All her gear fit easily into her backpack.

"Gosh," she said aloud as she zippered the pack shut. "Next week I'll be packing this with schoolbooks instead of camping clothes." For a moment she felt as sad as Stevie. It had been a wonderful, horse-filled summer, and it would be hard to go back to the routine of school. She sighed, but there was nothing she could do except make the best of it. *Anyway,* she thought as she picked up her backpack and hurried out to the car, *what better way to finish off a perfect summer than with a perfect, solar-powered weekend with Dad?*

ON THE OTHER side of town, Stevie and Lisa were preparing their own campsite in the hayloft above Belle's stall.

"What did you bring, Stevie?" Lisa stood on the ladder, her head poking up through the hayloft floor.

Stevie piled three game boxes on top of a hay bale. "I brought Monopoly if we want to play a long game, Scrabble if we want to test our brains, and two decks of cards if we want to try our luck at gin rummy." She pulled two other objects from her backpack. "Plus my little electronic game machine, my personal CD player, and two flashlights."

Lisa laughed. "Stevie, we've got electricity up here. There's a light switch on that wall behind you."

"I know. But I figured if we turned on the lights at night we might keep some of the horses awake. Better to use our flashlights and keep everything as normal as possible for them."

Lisa wondered how normal it would seem to the horses to have Stevie Lake playing gin rummy right above their heads all night, but she didn't say anything. Sometimes it was easier not to question Stevie's logic.

"Did you bring any clothes?" Lisa asked.

"Clothes?" Stevie frowned and looked through her backpack. "I don't know. I brought some horse magazines that I haven't had a chance to read yet, and I brought sixteen extra double-A batteries, in case anything goes dead." She looked up at Lisa. "No, I don't guess I brought any clothes."

"Don't you think you'll need some?"

"Yeah. But we can walk back home for clean clothes if we get really dirty, or if we find ourselves starving to death."

Lisa shook her head. "Don't tell me you didn't bring any food."

"I brought snacks and stuff for us to eat late at night. My mom said she'd fix us a tray of sandwiches later this afternoon." Stevie smiled as Lisa climbed the rest of the way up the ladder and threw her backpack and sleeping bag next to Stevie's. "What did you bring?"

"A change of clothes, toothpaste, and soap." Lisa shook her head. "Can you believe my mom actually wanted me to bring a first-aid kit and a weather radio? She acts as if we're going to be camping on Mount Everest instead of in the Pine Hollow hayloft."

"Well, your mom means well," Stevie said. She

31

knew that Mrs. Atwood could get some pretty strange ideas about making sure Lisa was properly equipped for every conceivable circumstance.

"Anyway, I threw in a notebook and pens, plus some bug spray and a new mystery I checked out of the library."

Stevie laughed. "Are you sure you'll want to read a mystery in a spooky old barn? Remember, Max says it gets pretty scary at night."

"Like you told him, Stevie, all that's just kid stuff."

Stevie looked around the loft. Her games, sleeping bag, and backpack were strewn across two hay bales, while Lisa's gear was neatly piled in the corner. "Well, I guess that's it for now. Looks just like home sweet home, doesn't it?"

Lisa nodded. "It sure does. Let's go get busy with some of the chores we promised to do. Then we can come back up here and have some fun!"

"Boy, THIS IS going to be great!" Colonel Hanson rolled down the window, letting the fragrant summer breeze blow through the front of the car. "I haven't been to this part of the Blue Ridge Mountains in years, but I bet it's as pretty as ever."

"When were you here last?" Carole smiled over at her dad.

"About fifteen years ago, with your mom." Colonel Hanson tuned the radio to his favorite oldies station. "I wonder if anything's changed."

"Probably not the important stuff," said Carole, thumbing through the field guides to Eastern forests and Eastern birds she'd brought along. She giggled. "I mean, they still probably have a lot of *Quercus albas* and *Mimus polyglottos*."

"Huh?" Her dad shot her a quizzical look.

"White oaks and mockingbirds," Carole answered with a laugh. "Those are their scientific names. It's right here on page twenty-two."

"Are you taking those books with you just to show up your dear old dad?" Colonel Hanson chuckled.

"No. I just wanted to see how many trees and birds I could identify. I know all the ones around Pine Hollow, but I bet we'll see some new ones up in the mountains."

"That's right." Colonel Hanson turned onto the highway that would take them to the mountains. "And don't forget we've got that telescope. You can watch birds with it during the day, and at night we can take it up to Mount Stringfellow."

Carole looked puzzled. "Mount Stringfellow?"

"Yes. It's very famous. On clear days, from the mountaintop, you can see all the way into West Virginia, and at night you can see a billion stars. If the nights are as clear as they're forecasting, we should be able to see the rings of Saturn."

"Really?" Carole said excitedly. She'd seen pictures of Saturn, but never the real thing.

"You bet."

"Wow." She settled back in the seat while one of her father's favorite old bebop tunes came on the radio. "The rings of Saturn. This is really going to be a wonderful trip."

In the early afternoon, they rolled into the parking lot closest to their campsite. Only a few other cars were parked there, and the thick, surrounding woods made civilization seem like a distant memory.

"Is our campsite far away?" Carole got out of the car and stretched her legs. She felt as if she'd been traveling for hours.

"It's about a mile that way." Colonel Hanson looked at his map and pointed straight up a mountain.

"Gosh, that's pretty far. Are we going to lug all this equipment up there?" Carole watched as her father unlocked the back of the station wagon. The thought of carrying the solar panels and the solar stove and the six different camping chairs up a mile-long hill was bad enough, but after they'd finished hauling all the stuff up there, they'd have to set it up. By then it would probably be time for them to go to bed.

"Oh, come on, Carole." Her dad smiled. "Remember? We're *semper fi.*"

"I know we can do it, Dad. I guess I'm just a little surprised that you would want to take all this high-tech equipment with you." She looked at her father. "I mean, you're a rough, tough Marine colonel. You don't need all this wimpy stuff."

Colonel Hanson laughed. "Well, that's true. I don't need all this stuff, and if I were with the troops, I wouldn't have any of it. But today I'm with my baby girl, and I want to make this the most wonderfully comfortable camping trip she's ever been on." He leaned over and gave Carole a hug. "In fact, honey, if I could spend my whole life making your life easy, I would."

"Thanks, Dad." Carole smiled and hugged him back. Even though lugging all this super-duper camping equipment a mile up a mountain was a little silly, she could go along with it. After all, her dad had planned this weekend just for her, and it was going to be a lot of fun, whether they were in cushy sleeping bags or not.

She looked at up him and gave a mock salute. "Just show me what you want me to carry, sir."

Her dad loaded her up with both backpacks, the sleeping bags, and a duffel bag full of the special camping clothes. He carried all the solar equipment, the tent, and the telescope. After two trips up and down the mountain trail, they stumbled into their campsite, tired and sweating.

"Gosh," Carole said, out of breath. "I thought we'd never get here."

"I know," huffed Colonel Hanson, dropping the rolled-up tent on the ground. "I think that map was wrong. I think it was more like three miles instead of one."

"It felt like about ten miles, straight up!" laughed Carole.

"Let's catch our breath for a minute, and then we'll set up camp."

They sat down on a fallen log bordering the small forest clearing that was to be their campsite. Colonel Hanson looked up at the tall trees surrounding them and frowned.

"You know, if we can't find a sunny spot around here, then we won't be able to charge that solar cell, and all our solar equipment will be useless."

Carole pointed through the trees. "It looks like there might be a bigger clearing over that way. Want me to go look?"

"Would you? You can scout for a sunny spot while I set up the tent. That way we'll be in business in time to have some fun before the sun goes down."

"Okay." Carole put the backpacks down and hopped off the log. "I'll be back in a flash."

"I'll be waiting for you, relaxing in our luxurious campsite," her father chuckled.

Carole set off through a tall stand of pine trees. Overhead a crow cawed from one of the top limbs. Carole looked up and smiled.

"Wonder if you're *Cronius crokus*?" she asked as the bird tilted its head and peered down at her. She'd have to look up crows in her book when she got back to camp. She walked a short distance farther, finally reaching the bright spot in the forest. It was a campsite that no one was using, and sunlight beamed down on rich green grass, making the air feel warm and dry.

"This looks like a perfect place for solar panels," she said aloud. "It's big enough, and certainly bright enough." She'd just turned to hurry back to her dad when she thought she heard a very familiar noise. Like the crow, she cocked her head to one side and listened again. There, floating on the breeze, was the undeniable neigh of a horse!

Unbelievable, thought Carole. *What kind of horse would be way up here?* Quickly she turned and walked in the direction the sound had come from. Her father was still probably trying to figure out how to pitch the fancy tent—he wouldn't be worried about the solar panel location for a while.

She followed a slight trail that meandered through the trees and along the ridge of the mountains. About a quarter mile away, she saw it: A large green tent was pitched in a little clearing in the woods, and just to one side was a makeshift paddock of nylon rope strung around three tall pine trees.

"Oh!" Carole cried in surprise. Inside the paddock stood two Appaloosas, both of which were looking directly at her. One was mostly white with brown spots, while the other was a strawberry roan. Smiling, she hurried down the trail. Why not say hello, especially when your next-door neighbors were horses?

"Hi, guys!" she said softly as she approached the paddock.

Both horses stepped forward as if eager to be greeted. Carole rubbed their noses. The spotted one nudged up close to her, while the roan arched his neck, just like a cat. They seemed to love the attention. Carole was wishing she had thought to bring some carrots when suddenly the flaps on the green tent opened.

A bald man of average height came out. He wore black jeans and a long duster. A woman came out just behind him. She was blond and wore a red spangled cowboy shirt.

"Hello," the man said to Carole. "Can I help you?"

"Oh, I was just saying hi to your horses," Carole explained with a friendly smile. "My dad and I are setting up our tent two campsites over. I was looking for a sunny spot for some solar panels and heard your pals here."

The man and the woman continued to stare at her, unspeaking.

"Uh, my name's Carole Hanson, from Willow Creek, Virginia."

"We're the Loftins from Henderson, Pennsylvania," the woman replied.

Carole smiled. "Do you camp with your horses a lot? Back home I ride almost every day."

"We camp with them as much as we can," the man said, still not cracking a smile.

"Well," Carole said, suddenly feeling as if these people weren't the least bit interested in striking up a conversation. "I guess I'd better be getting back up the mountain. My dad will be wondering what happened to me." She gave the roan's nose a final rub. "Looks like you have some wonderful camping companions."

"That's right." The woman gave the barest of smiles. "We do."

Carole hurried back up the path. Most horsepeople she met were friendly, even eager to talk about their horses. These two acted as if they were carved out of rock! *Oh, well,* she thought as she neared her campsite. *I guess horsepeople come in as many temperaments as horses do.*

She found her father relaxing in a camping armchair in front of their tent. The tent was bright orange and looked so much like a giant mushroom that Carole could barely keep from laughing.

"Hi," she called with a giggle. "Guess what I found?"

"A sunny spot for the solar panels?"

"Yes, but guess what else?"

"What?"

"Two Appaloosas. They're over at the campsite past the next one. Their owners aren't the friendliest people in the world, but the horses were great!"

40

Colonel Hanson shook his head and started to laugh. "Carole, you're the only person on the planet who would go looking for a sunny clearing on the top of a mountain and find two horses instead!"

Carole shrugged. "I guess when your horse radar gets going, it's hard to turn it off."

Colonel Hanson stood up and stretched his arms over his head. "Well, I'm glad you made some new four-legged friends. But now that you're back, I think I'll go set up those panels, then dig out a latrine."

"Good idea, Dad," Carole said. "I knew we'd put some of your old Marine Corps habits to good use while we were up here. How about I start supper while you dig?"

"Deal!" said Colonel Hanson. "Do you think you can figure out how to use the solar oven? It's already charged up."

"I think so," replied Carole. "If I can't, I'll just call my local solar expert, who happens to be close by."

Colonel Hanson lifted a small shovel over his shoulder and walked several yards downhill from their camp. In the meantime, Carole began to cook supper. Her dad had piled all the other camping equipment behind the tent, so she had to search a minute before she found the solar refrigerator. She took some cold chicken they'd brought from home, put it inside the solar oven, and turned the dial to 325°F. The oven made a strange chirping sound, but then a red light came on and the thing began to heat up. While the chicken was warming, she found their camp table and covered it with a cloth, then set up their chairs, adding two citronella candles to keep the bugs away. By the time her father returned from his digging, the candles were lit and the table was laden with a bowl of potato chips, two big glasses of fruit juice, and a plate of brownies for dessert.

"Hey, Carole, this looks great!" her father exclaimed.

"If the solar oven does what it's supposed to do, then the chicken should be ready just about now." Carol put on a mitt and opened the oven door. Amazingly, the chicken was hot and toasty brown, just as if she'd heated it up in their oven at home. Of course, they could have eaten it cold in half the time, but she didn't guess that mattered. Her father was so proud of the solar oven that she was happy to use it.

She carried the chicken to the table, and they both sat down to eat.

"Mmmm," Colonel Hanson said after he took his first bite. "This is wonderful. I guess that solar oven did okay, huh?"

"It was great, Dad." Carole smiled. "It was lots of fun to use."

"I think eating outside makes everything taste twice as good."

"I think eating after you've hiked three miles, two

of them uphill, makes everything taste three times as good," Carole added.

Her father laughed. "Maybe it's a combination of both."

They were both so hungry they finished all the chicken and potato chips, then half the plate of brownies. By the time they got the dishes cleaned up, the sun was just beginning to drop behind the tops of the tallest trees.

"Hey, how about heading up to Mount Stringfellow?" Colonel Hanson asked. He checked his watch. "We've still got another half hour before sunset."

Carole pointed to a cluster of dark purple clouds in the northern sky. "Look at all those clouds. Do you think it might rain?"

"Well, let's see." Colonel Hanson went into the tent and came back out with a small instrument in a red leather case. He faced the setting sun and squinted at the dial. "According to this electronic barometer, we've got nothing but high pressure all around us." He snapped the case shut and grinned at Carole. "Those clouds don't mean rain. They just mean that we'll have an even more beautiful sunset to enjoy."

"That's a relief," said Carole.

"You grab a couple of flashlights and the map, and I'll get the telescope. We'll have to hurry if we want to get to the top of Mount Stringfellow by sunset."

43

"How far is it?" Carole didn't know if she was up for another hard climb, especially in the dark.

Her dad pointed to a high mountain that loomed behind her. "Oh, just over there. I think the trail's about half a mile long, but the rangers keep the path clear."

"Okay," said Carole. "I'm game if you are. Mount Stringfellow, here we come!"

5

"HERE COMES DINNER!"

Stevie's voice floated up from the bottom of the ladder. A second later Lisa saw the edge of what looked like a tray come poking up through the trapdoor of the hayloft.

"Do you need some help, Stevie?" she called.

"Yes. Grab the end of this tray so these sandwiches won't slide off."

Lisa crawled across the soft hay and grasped the end of the long, skinny tray that Stevie was trying to push up the ladder. "Okay," she called. "I've got it. Just let me pull it up from here."

"Okay."

Stevie let go of the tray and Lisa carefully pulled it through the trapdoor. She put it down against the

45

back wall of the hayloft, far away from where either of them might accidentally step on it. When she had it positioned safely, she looked at it and gasped. Under a thick layer of plastic wrap were about twenty sandwiches, all cut into fancy little triangles. Lisa could see ham and cheese, turkey and cheese, bologna and cheese, and peanut butter and jelly.

"Thanks!" Stevie's head poked up through the trapdoor. "That was a real case of four hands being better than two."

"Did your mom make all this food for us?" Lisa asked in amazement.

"Sure." Stevie climbed the rest of the way up the ladder. "That's our dinner." She rattled a shoebox that she had tucked under one arm. "And this is our dessert. Two dozen chocolate coconut surprises."

"Stevie, this is enough food to feed ten people."

"Think so?" Stevie looked surprised. "I asked Mom to make extra. I figured we'd eat now, but we might get hungry again around midnight. Then we might need an early-morning snack at four A.M., then some emergency might happen that we'd need some extra nourishment for, and then we might want to eat some for breakfast in the morning." She plopped down beside the sandwich tray. "If you multiply two people times five possible feedings, then I suppose it is like feeding ten people at once."

Lisa tried to figure out Stevie's logic, but as usual, it

eluded her. All she knew was that Stevie had brought more sandwiches up there than they could possibly eat.

"Shall we have dinner now?" Stevie asked.

Lisa nodded. "Actually, I'm pretty hungry."

"Me too." Stevie began to unwrap the sandwiches, then stopped. "Oh, rats!" she exclaimed. "I forgot to bring anything to drink."

"I'll go down to the refrigerator and get a couple of sodas," Lisa said.

"Great," said Stevie. "I'll fix our plates."

Lisa climbed down the ladder and hurried to the office, where she got two cold cans of soda and scribbled an IOU on the memo pad attached to the refrigerator door. By the time she got back to the hayloft, Stevie had their plates arranged—each with a sandwich, chips, and two chocolate coconut surprises.

"Here." Stevie held out one plate to Lisa. "I gave you a turkey and cheese and bologna and cheese."

"Thanks." Lisa smiled. "Everything looks great."

They relaxed in the hay and began to eat. Below them they could hear Belle munching on her hay, and next to her Starlight was noisily slurping water.

"Sounds like this is dinnertime for everybody at Pine Hollow, doesn't it?" giggled Stevie, reaching for her second sandwich.

"I feel just like one of the horses," said Lisa with a laugh. "Eating in the hay and sleeping in the hayloft."

She took a sip of soda, then reached in her backpack for her pencil and paper. "I'm going to make a list of all the chores we need to do tomorrow. I'd hate to get so involved in one thing that we forget to do something else. We don't want to disappoint Max."

"That's a good idea," Stevie said as she retrieved another sandwich. "And don't forget, we promised Carole we'd take extra-special care of Starlight."

Lisa looked at Stevie and frowned. "Maybe we ought to tackle some of these chores tonight. That way we'll have less to do tomorrow. Maybe we could even go for a ride in the afternoon."

"Oh, they'll wait," Stevie said, her mouth full. "We don't absolutely have to do anything right this second." She crunched a potato chip and thought a minute. "Although I guess we could groom Starlight tonight. He would enjoy it, and we've got enough time before dark."

Lisa smiled. "Why don't we do that as soon as we finish eating?"

"Okay," said Stevie, turning back to the sandwich tray.

In a few minutes they were through. Lisa put their dirty paper plates in a bag she'd brought for garbage, then put the soda cans aside to be recycled. She was about to close up the chocolate coconut surprises when she caught a glimpse of the sandwich tray. It was almost empty.

"Stevie!" she cried, astonished. "Did we actually eat all these sandwiches?"

Stevie crawled over and looked at the tray. "Well, you ate two and I ate—uh, I guess I lost count after the third." She grinned and patted her stomach. "It's amazing how hungry taking care of twenty-five horses can make you."

Lisa looked at her friend. "Would that be anything like 'eating like a horse'?"

Stevie shrugged and laughed. "In this case it's more like eating *for* a horse. Only it's twenty-five horses instead of just one."

"Oh, Stevie." Lisa shook her head with a sigh.

"Well, now I'm ready to give Starlight the most energetic grooming he's ever had!"

The girls covered their meager leftovers with plastic wrap and climbed down the ladder. Most of the horses were standing quietly in their stalls, either dozing on their feet or idly chewing small mouthfuls of hay. When the girls opened Starlight's stall, they found him awake but wearing a heavy-lidded, sleepy look.

"I think he might have been drifting off to sleep," Lisa whispered.

"That's okay," replied Stevie. "This will be just like a body massage. After this grooming he'll probably fall asleep the minute we leave his stall."

The girls got brushes and currycombs and each took one side of Starlight. He seemed surprised to have two people grooming him at the same time, but he stood calmly and gave a little nicker of pleasure. Soon they had his deep mahogany coat shining and all the tangles worked out of his dark mane.

"Think we can skip the hoof polish, since all he's going to do is go to sleep?" asked Lisa.

"I think so," said Stevie. "But we'll do that, too, before Carole gets back."

Lisa gave Starlight a pat. "I wonder what Carole's doing right now?"

"Probably roasting marshmallows with her dad." Stevie wiped the front of Starlight's nose with a soft cloth. "Starlight, your person is out with her father right now, but she'll be back on Monday, so don't worry."

Lisa giggled at Starlight's utterly passive expression. "He doesn't look worried at all."

"Well, you never know. I just wanted to reassure him that life would return to normal."

"Then you should announce that on the PA system. All these horses are probably wondering why two people are suddenly sleeping in their hayloft." Lisa glanced over at Starlight's water bucket. "Look, he's almost finished his water. I'll go bring him some more and put some fresh hay in his crib while you finish up."

Lisa went to get more hay and water while Stevie put the last touches on Starlight's grooming. A few moments later he stood there gleaming, with both his water bucket and hay crib full.

"Good night, Starlight," Stevie called.

"Sleep tight," added Lisa with a giggle. "Don't let the bedbugs bite!"

"Speaking of sleeping tight, how about we go back to the loft?" Stevie said with a yawn. "I know it's early, but I guess when you sleep with horses, you feel like going to bed when they do."

"Suits me," said Lisa.

They climbed back into the loft and spread their sleeping bags out next to each other. Lisa read for a few minutes, and Stevie played one of her electronic games, but soon they found their own eyelids drooping.

"I think I'm going to sleep," yawned Stevie. "We'll have a hectic enough day tomorrow. We may as well be rested for it."

"Right," said Lisa, catching Stevie's yawn. She closed her book and zipped up her sleeping bag. "Good night, Stevie."

"Good night, Lisa," Stevie replied. "Good night, Belle and Starlight," she whispered through the cracks in the floor, just before she turned over and closed her eyes to sleep.

"COME ON, DAD! If you hurry, we can make it!" Carole bounded ahead of her father to the top of Mount

Stringfellow, just in time to see the last rays of sunlight disappear behind a stunning pink-and-purple cloud bank. For a minute the whole mountaintop was bathed in a soft violet glow; then the sun slipped beneath the horizon and the light faded to dusk.

"Did you see that sunset?" Carole asked as her father came trotting up the path, carrying the telescope over one shoulder.

"I think I saw the grand finale about fifty feet below, through the trees." Colonel Hanson's breath came heavily.

Carole sighed. "It was so beautiful! If we'd gotten up here about five minutes earlier, we could have seen the whole thing from here. At least we saw most of it on the way up."

Colonel Hanson surveyed the darkening sky around the top of the mountain. "Now we won't have to wait as long for the stars. I hear they come out up here fast, just like flashbulbs at a rock concert."

"Is that so?" Carole couldn't help smiling at her father's choice of words. He sounded as if he were more at home at rock concerts than on a Marine Corps base.

"Yep." Colonel Hanson grinned. "Let's set up the telescope so we can see them up close."

Carole turned in a circle. The bare top of the mountain offered a long-range view for miles in every direction. "Which way should we point it?"

"Let's try east," Colonel Hanson suggested, walking over to the opposite side of the mountaintop from where the sun went down. "Planets usually follow the path of the sun, more or less, so they should rise in the east, just like it does."

Carole followed her father and held the body of the telescope steady while he adjusted the legs. He aimed the lens at a point in the distant sky and smiled at Carole.

"You take the first watch," he said, pointing to an eyepiece on the side of the telescope.

Carole bent over and looked through the lens. She expected to see a million tiny lights twinkling, but all she saw was a circle of dark gray.

"I can't see anything," she said, disappointed.

"Let me have a look," Colonel Hanson replied. "Maybe it's not adjusted right."

Carole moved back and let her father have a turn. "Hmm," she heard him say. "I see something, but it's nothing like a star." He tilted the telescope to the right. "There it is again. . . . It's a big cloud bank!"

He straightened up and frowned at Carole. "I don't get it. I checked the electronic barometer twice before we came up here. It showed no signs of a front coming through, yet I'm seeing a whole bunch of clouds."

"Maybe a fast storm system's moving in. We learned about those in the meteorology unit of earth science last year."

"I don't think that's possible with the barometer reading as high as it was." Colonel Hanson shook his head. "I think it must be just a quick-moving part of a 'partly cloudy' forecast. Why don't we sit down and wait for it to clear?"

"Okay," said Carole. She was happy to be up on Mount Stringfellow. It was beautiful, with or without the stars. She sat down close to the telescope, and her father sat beside her.

"Want to tell knock-knock jokes?" he asked.

"No, Dad. That's Stevie's thing. Let's play a game. Let's take turns naming all the movies with one-name titles."

"Okay," Colonel Hanson chuckled. "You go first."

"*Amistad,*" said Carole.

"*Rocky,*" her father replied.

"*Mulan,*" Carole shot back.

"*Indiscreet.*" Colonel Hanson laughed.

"*In the Street?*" Carole frowned. "Dad, that's three words."

"No, Carole. *I-n-d-i-s-c-r-e-e-t. Indiscreet.* Cary Grant and Ingrid Bergman."

"The movies have to be from the age of sound, Dad," Carole warned with a grin.

"That one is—it's from 1958."

"Well, then, the last twenty-five years. Something I could have seen on the late show."

"Okay, okay."

The night remained dark and without stars. Carole and her dad played on, laughing, almost forgetting about the telescope altogether. Finally Carole saw something on the distant horizon.

"Look!" she said, rising to her feet. At first she was afraid it was something ominous, like a thundercloud, but then she realized her father had been right. What she was seeing was the last edge of a cloud cover, and the breeze that had suddenly begun to blow across Mount Stringfellow was sweeping the clouds ahead of it.

"I think it's going to clear up!" she cried.

They stepped back over to the telescope. When they looked up just a few minutes later, the sky was filled with a billion glorious stars, twinkling just like camera flashes at a rock concert, only never going out.

"Oh, wow!" Carole breathed.

"Now we're cooking," said Colonel Hanson. "Let's see what we can bring into focus."

Carole lay on her back and looked up into the sky while her father adjusted the focus on the telescope. She felt as if the stars were so close she could reach out and touch them.

"*Awwrriiiight!*" her father cried. "Carole! Come have a look at this!"

Carole hurried over to the telescope. She looked through the eyepiece, expecting to see more glittering stars. Instead she saw a beautiful yellow planet with deep silver rings around it. "Gosh," she cried, "the rings of Saturn!"

"Pretty impressive, huh?" Her father asked, smiling.

"I can't believe that's really Saturn. And I'm actually seeing it right now, with my own eyes!"

"You sure are. The light that we're seeing from Saturn right now left the planet back when we were having supper. It takes a little over an hour to get to Earth. Want to see if we can find Jupiter?"

"Absolutely!"

Carole stepped back to let her father readjust the telescope.

"Can you name the planets of the solar system in order?" he asked as he turned the knobs on the eyepiece.

"Uh, I used to be able to, but I get confused after Jupiter," Carole admitted.

Colonel Hanson grinned. "Just remember My Very Educated Mother Just Showed Us Nine Planets."

" 'My very educated mother . . .' " Carole frowned a moment, then smiled. "Oh, I get it. Mercury, Venus, Earth, Mars, Jupiter, Saturn, Uranus, Neptune, and Pluto. Cool, Dad. Now I'll never forget again."

"Okay, come have a look at this."

Carole looked through the eyepiece again. This time, instead of a yellow planet with silver rings, she saw a huge golden striped ball with a pink swirl on one side. "Wow! Is that Jupiter?"

"None other."

"It's so big!" she cried. "It practically fills the whole lens."

"It's the biggest planet in the solar system," her father explained. "In fact, the gravitational pull of Jupiter helps keep Earth in her orbit. How's that for a big ecosystem?"

"Unbelievable," breathed Carole.

They looked at the stars for the rest of the evening, finding Mars and Venus and some nebulae that could be seen only with a telescope. Carole could have stargazed forever, but when Colonel Hanson checked his watch and saw that it was eleven o'clock, he suggested they turn in.

"I think we'd better go back to our camp now, honey," he said. "It's been a long day, and it's time for us to hit the hay."

"I thought we were hitting the solar-powered down, Dad," Carole teased.

"Hay, down, whatever," her father replied.

Though she hadn't realized it till then, Carole actually was pretty tired. "I guess you're right, although stargazing really makes the time fly by." She smiled at her father. "This was one of the best nights I've spent in my entire life!"

"Me too, honey." Colonel Hanson smiled. "And we'll have several more. Right now, however, it's time to turn in. If you'll light the way down the trail, I'll carry the telescope. Get my solar flashlight over there."

Carole ran to where her father pointed and picked up his solar flashlight. She turned it on, expecting a bright beam, but all she got was a dim flicker, then darkness.

"Guess what, Dad?" she said with a laugh. "Looks like your solar power set with the sun." She clicked on her own flashlight, into which she'd just put fresh D batteries. "But my old battery-operated one works just fine!"

"Guess you can't improve on everything," her father said with a laugh as she lit their way down the mountain.

CRAAAAACK !

Stevie and Lisa bolted upright in their sleeping bags at the same time, each blinking at the other in the dim hayloft.

Craaaack—splat. Craaack, craaack, craaack! Splat, splat, splat! Then—the high yip of a horse in pain.

"Stevie!" Lisa cried. "What's going on?"

"I don't know." Stevie hurriedly unzipped her sleeping bag. "But that was Belle. I'd know her voice anywhere."

Stevie leaped up from the hay and crawled down the ladder. Lisa followed close behind. They switched on the light in Belle's stall and peeked over the door. The pretty bay mare was standing there with several CD cases scattered around her left foreleg.

"What on earth?" Stevie blinked as she hurried into the stall. She rubbed Belle's nose and felt her legs, making sure the startled horse had not been injured.

"Is she okay?" Lisa asked.

"I think so," Stevie replied. "But she's as mystified as I am. She doesn't find CDs in her stall every day."

Lisa gathered the cases up while Stevie calmed Belle. They were all Stevie's—mostly the heavy metal music she'd brought with her—but how had they gotten into Belle's stall? Frowning, Lisa looked up at the ceiling. There, exactly where Stevie's feet would have been in the hayloft, was a hole big enough for the CDs to fit through.

"I know what happened," Lisa said, pointing to the ceiling. "You must have kicked them through that hole in your sleep."

Stevie peered up at the hayloft. "Well, I was having a dream about dancing sandwiches."

"Dancing sandwiches?" Lisa blinked.

"Yeah. The turkey and cheeses were waltzing with the chocolate coconut surprises." Stevie shrugged. "Maybe I overdid it a little at dinner last night."

"Oh, Stevie," said Lisa. "What if these CDs had fallen in some other horse's stall? What if another horse had gotten hurt?"

"I know." Stevie shuddered. "We were awfully

60

lucky. Although Belle does have a little bump on her withers. Look."

Lisa watched as Stevie gently pressed a small swelling at the top of Belle's shoulder. Belle flinched and again gave a short squeal of pain.

"Poor baby," Stevie whispered, wrapping her arms around Belle's neck. "I'm so sorry. I promise nothing like that will ever happen again."

Belle nickered in reply.

"I think she's okay," Stevie said.

"Then let's turn out her light so that she can get back to sleep," suggested Lisa. "And we can do the same."

"Okay." Stevie gave Belle a final hug and turned out the light. Then both girls climbed back up the ladder. Lisa gave Stevie her CDs to store in a safe place.

"Maybe I'll put them at the top of my sleeping bag instead of the bottom," said Stevie. "Surely I won't head-butt any off the hayloft in my sleep."

"Not unless you start dreaming about sandwiches playing soccer," Lisa giggled.

"Speaking of sandwiches"—Stevie sat up again—"are you hungry?"

"No." Lisa sat up, too. "But I'm not sleepy anymore, either."

"Me neither." Stevie reached for the tray of

wrapped sandwiches. "Maybe a little snack will help me get sleepy again."

Stevie ate another sandwich while Lisa made some notes on her to-do list. Then Stevie listened to one of her CDs while Lisa played Stevie's electronic game.

"Are you sleepy yet?" Lisa asked after she'd killed off a hundred space raiders and saved planet Earth.

"What?" Stevie said loudly, holding out one earphone.

"I said, are you sleepy yet?"

Stevie shook her head. "I don't think we should have had those sodas with dinner. They supposedly have a lot of caffeine."

"Well, we had to drink something," Lisa said. Suddenly she tilted her head to the floor below. "Listen!"

Stevie took her headphones off and tilted her head, too. Belle was shifting in her straw, having her own dream. The girls could hear the soft rasp of her breathing, broken by an occasional half whinny.

Stevie grinned. "Wonder what she's dreaming about?"

"Dancing apples?" Lisa said with a giggle.

"You know, I don't think I've ever heard the stable this quiet," Stevie whispered.

"Me neither," said Lisa. "It's kind of neat, isn't it?"

Stevie nodded, and they both lay in their sleeping bags listening to the horses and talking quietly. They fell asleep only when dawn rose up over the Virginia hills.

MILES AWAY, SNUG in a sleeping bag deep in the Virginia wilderness, Carole awoke with a start. She was almost certain she'd just heard the soft whinny of a horse. *You must have been dreaming about Pine Hollow*, she told herself, but she sat up anyway. Though she was in the forest camping in a state-of-the-art tent, she was sure the sound had been real. Being careful not to disturb her sleeping father, she crawled out of her sleeping bag and stepped through the tent door. She smiled. There, just at the edge of their campsite, stood the shadowy form of the strawberry roan Appaloosa she'd met the day before.

His ears pricked up the moment he saw her. Slowly she began to walk toward him. He seemed happy to see her and took a few steps in her direction.

"Hi, boy," she whispered as he came up and sniffed the top of her head. "What are you doing out so late?"

He arched his neck to be petted, just as he had before. She giggled as she scratched him behind his ears. "You're being very naughty to take a nighttime jaunt like this. Now I've got to figure out a way to get you back."

The roan nodded as if to agree. Carole laughed again. This was a mischievous horse, but he was gentle and affectionate, too. He was wearing the same halter he'd had on earlier. If she could just find some rope, she could lead him back to his paddock in the trees.

She turned and walked over to the mass of camping equipment that was stacked behind their tent. Surely in all this high-tech stuff there would be a rope. As she felt along the table they'd set up for dinner, her fingers curled around a long piece of twine that her father had used to tie some equipment together.

"This should work," she whispered.

She grabbed her flashlight from the table and hurried back to the horse, tying one end of the twine to his halter. It was the thinnest lead rope she'd ever used, but it would have to do.

"Come on, boy," she said, clucking gently. "Let's go back home."

She led the horse back in the direction he'd come from. Though her flashlight gave out a bright light, the thick trees made it especially hard to see. When she shined her light toward the ground, she got thunked in the head by a low branch. When she shined her light up at the trees, she stumbled over rocks and gnarled roots. The horse walked calmly beside her, never missing one step.

"It must be nice to have eyes that can see in the dark," Carole grumbled as a prickly shrub grabbed at her arm.

When she nearly tripped over an old rotten log, she gave up.

"Okay," she said. "I promised myself I wouldn't do this, but I think it's the only way I'm going to get you home without killing myself."

She stopped the horse, climbed on the log, then hoisted herself onto his back. The roan stood still, calm and willing.

"Okay," Carole said, holding one end of the rope and the horse's mane. "I know you know the way. Let's go home."

In just a few moments the roan had picked his way through the forest, back to his camp. The Loftins' green tent was dark, its flaps down. Apparently they were still asleep, unaware that one of their horses had wandered in the night.

No need to wake them up, either, thought Carole as she slid off the roan's back and led him to his paddock. One of the top nylon ropes that made the fence had come loose, allowing him an easy jump to freedom. The other horse watched with interest as she led the roan back over the collapsed rope and into his makeshift home.

"Now, you guys behave yourselves for the rest of the night," she whispered as she retied the rope securely to the tree. She pointed her finger at the roan. "And no more midnight rambles for you!"

He looked so serious that she had to laugh. He was

a great horse and would probably be a lot of fun to own. "Bye now," she called. She clicked her flashlight back on and walked carefully up the trail to her own campsite, wishing she had a horse with night vision on her return journey.

"YOU WON'T BELIEVE what happened last night, Dad," Carole said as she followed her father out of the tent and into the bright morning light.

"What?"

"One of those horses I met yesterday escaped from his paddock and came over here. I woke up and had to take him back to his campsite."

"Really?" Colonel Hanson's eyes grew wide. "Why didn't you wake me up? I could have helped."

"You were sleeping so soundly. It just didn't seem like that big a deal. I tied a rope to his halter and started leading him, although I wound up having to ride him through the dark trees."

Colonel Hanson shook his head. "I didn't even know horses could be ridden through the forest at night. Maybe it's just as well you took care of it. How about I fire up the cookstove and make breakfast? We can celebrate Carole Hanson's famous horse rescue with a big stack of pancakes."

Carole grinned. "Sounds great to me! I'll go wash up in the creek while you cook."

Carole tidied up their tent, wincing as her father

crashed around among the boxes of cooking equipment outside.

"Are you sure you don't need any help?" she called.

"No, I'm fine. You go on down to the creek and wash up. I'll have the pancakes done by the time you get back."

"Okay." She took a small toiletry kit and a towel down to the little creek that ran close to their tent. A chorus of yellow warblers serenaded her as she splashed the cold creek water on her face. By the time she had finished brushing her teeth and combing her hair, her stomach was growling, so she packed up her things and hurried back to their tent.

She found her father standing in the middle of the equipment, a frazzled look on his face. "Is it pancakes yet, Dad?" she called.

"Uh, not quite," Colonel Hanson answered, his mouth pulled down in a puzzled frown.

"Need some help?" Carole tossed her things inside the tent and went over to the solar cookstove. The grilling surface was red hot, sending rays of heat shimmering into the air.

"Well, I can't seem to find the pancake recipe." Her father scratched his head. "Or the pancake bowl, or even the pancake flipper. But I've got the syrup!" he announced.

"Maybe I can find the other stuff." Carole got down on her hands and knees and began to sift through the half-dozen boxes that lay piled behind their tent. In the first one she found the pancake flipper, then the set of collapsible bowls. She never did see a recipe, but she did find some pancake mix.

"Here," she said. "All you need to do is add water to this."

"Thanks!" Colonel Hanson grinned. "Now I'll have these babies cooked in no time!"

He measured out enough pancake mix and began to stir everything together. "Okay. Now, if you'll hand me the butter . . ."

"The butter?" Carole blinked.

"Yes. The butter. So the pancakes won't stick to the griddle."

"I don't think we have any butter, Dad." She checked the refrigerator to be sure, but she was right. They had coffee, orange juice, sodas, apples, jam, and pancake syrup, but not one stick of butter. "Sorry," she said with a shrug. "I guess we forgot the butter."

"Oh well," said Colonel Hanson. "This grill is so hot we probably won't need any. I'll just pour these things on here and flip 'em real quick and they proba-bly won't stick at all."

Carole didn't say anything. She'd never seen a pan-cake cooked like that, but maybe her dad had some secret Marine Corps trick she didn't know. She watched as he poured four circles of batter onto the sizzling stove top.

"Okay," he said confidently. "Where's the flipper?"

"Right here." She handed it to him quickly.

Tiny bubbles were already forming on the first pancake. It was time to turn it over. Colonel Hanson scooted the flipper under one edge and gave a quick twist upward, but instead of flipping in midair, half of the blackened pancake just flopped over and collapsed across the raw side. It looked awful.

"Okay." Colonel Hanson shook his head. "That one was just a test. Let's go on to number two."

He went to work on the other pancakes, trying to pry them up before they burned. The whole batch went the same way: Some flipped and then burned, others burned before they could be flipped. By the time he'd used up all the batter, he had a grand stack of three pancakes that looked vaguely edible.

Colonel Hanson looked sadly at the mound of charred pancakes. "I didn't think pancakes would be quite so much trouble."

"Don't worry, Dad," Carole reassured him. "We've got lots of syrup. They'll taste great."

They divided the pancakes in half. Carole doused hers with syrup, and Colonel Hanson ate his with some blueberry jam.

"Mmm," Colonel Hanson said, an odd look on his face. "Aren't they good?"

Though Carole's pancake tasted somewhere between burned toast and soggy cereal, she tried to

69

smile. "They've really got the flavor of the outdoors," she said, forcing down the gummy, burned dough. "You know, Dad," she said, changing the subject with a gulp, "I really loved looking at the stars last night. Those planets were unbelievable."

"They were terrific, weren't they?" Colonel Hanson laughed, trying hard to swallow his own pancake. "Want to go again tonight?"

"Sure," Carole agreed eagerly. "But what are we going to do in the meantime?"

"Well, I was hoping we could get in some early-morning fishing, but since our pancake breakfast took a little longer than expected, I guess we could get in some late-morning fishing. I've got Colonel Cheatham's collapsible canoe and paddle. Does that sound like fun?"

"Sure does." Carole smiled, washing the last bite of her pancakes down with a big glass of milk.

By the time they got the dishes cleared away, it was nearly noon. Colonel Hanson eagerly accepted Carole's offer to make sandwiches for the fishing trip. Without the solar cookstove to haul, they had only the collapsible boat, the folding paddles, and an enormous box of lures and tackle to take along. With her plain old cane pole slung over her shoulder, Carole helped her dad lug all the equipment to the creek.

"Uh, D-Dad?" Carole stammered when they came

to the bank of a small creek. "It looks awfully small for canoeing."

"Well, sometimes they just seem that way." Her father grinned. "Don't worry. It'll be great. Colonel Cheatham says these boats can float in a teaspoon of water."

"But Dad . . ."

"Don't worry, Carole," her father said as he began to unfold the boat. "Trust me."

She put down her fishing tackle and helped him. The little canvas-and-aluminum boat unfolded easily, as did both its paddles. Colonel Hanson pushed the canoe out into the water, where it bobbed, awaiting its passengers.

"See? Plenty of water to keep us afloat. Now, ladies first," said Colonel Hanson with a bow.

"That's okay, Dad." Carole smiled. "I'll let you go first."

"Okay." Colonel Hanson put his hands on either side of the boat and slowly crept forward. The little canoe wobbled for a moment, then floated easily on the water. "There. See? It's great. Grab those paddles and climb aboard!"

Carole handed the paddles to her father and stepped into the boat just as he had. It wobbled beneath her until she crawled onto the seat.

"See?" Colonel Hanson said. "Easy, isn't it?"

Carole nodded. "Where are we going?"

Colonel Hanson dipped his paddle into the water. "Let's see if we can get close to that big tree. I bet some old bass is down in that dark water, just waiting to be caught."

"Okay, Dad." Carole dipped her paddle into the water on the other side of the canoe and made a single stroke. The canoe went forward for about ten seconds, then suddenly turned sideways. Colonel Hanson swayed to the left in his seat. The little boat gave a shudder, and the next thing Carole knew the canoe was over their heads and she was sitting on the creek bottom, under water.

She came up coughing and spewing water. Her father was on the other side of the canoe, water pouring from his fishing hat as if a bucket had overturned on his head.

"Are you all right, Carole?" her father cried.

"I'm fine," she replied, starting to laugh. "The water's just barely above my waist. But look at your hat!"

Colonel Hanson took the hat off and wrung it out like a rag. "What happened?" he asked. "We were doing so great!"

"I don't know." Carole wiped the water from her eyes. "Let's get back on the bank and figure it out."

Together they shoved the capsized canoe to the side of the creek. Carole's once dry clothes now clung to her in a soggy mess, and she could feel mud squishing

72

inside her shoes. Walking back up the trail like this was going to feel awful!

They emptied the swamped canoe and dragged it onto the bank. Colonel Hanson hopped up on the bank and offered Carole his hand. "I'm sorry, honey. Are you sure you're okay?"

"Yes, Dad, I'm fine. Just a little damp." Carole wrung the water out of her shirttail and eyed the soaked canoe. "You know, since I just have this cane pole, maybe I'll let you fish from the canoe by yourself. I'm just as happy fishing from the bank, and I know how much you want to try that collapsible boat."

"Oh, I don't know." Her father shrugged and grinned sheepishly. "Maybe it's meant for deeper water. Anyway, fishing from the bank has always been a more exciting way to catch fish."

"Drier, too," Carole added with a giggle.

They left the collapsible canoe in a waterlogged heap and squished over to the big tree. Carole carried her cane pole while her Dad took a graphite rod with a vast array of lures and flies. They sat on one of the huge tree roots that overhung the creek.

"What are you fishing with today?" Colonel Hanson asked as he opened his tackle box.

"A worm, I suppose," Carole said. Worms were what she had always fished with. There was no reason to change now.

"You want me to find one for you and bait your hook?" Colonel Hanson asked.

"No thanks, Dad. I can do it." Carole hopped off the root and dug around in the soft earth beneath the tree. In a moment she found several long, crawling worms. *Ugh,* she thought as she picked the longest one up. *I don't remember them being quite this squirmy.* Carefully she grabbed her fishhook in one hand and held the worm in the other. She didn't like the idea of having to thread the sharp hook through the worm's body, but she didn't want to admit that to her father. She wished she could close her eyes, but she didn't dare do that if she wanted to avoid piercing her own thumb with the hook. *Yuck!* She thought. *This is really not as much fun as I remembered.* Taking a deep breath, she open her eyes wide and threaded the worm on the hook as quickly as she could. Then she swung her line out into the middle of the creek.

For the next several hours they fished, or in Carole's case, drowned a helpless worm. Colonel Hanson spent most of his time either adjusting his line or changing his lures. By the time they ate their sandwiches, neither had had a single nibble, and by the time the mosquitoes came out for their own dinner in the late afternoon, Colonel Hanson was ready to call it quits.

"I don't know about you, but I'm exhausted," he

said, reeling in his line for the final time. "I wonder where all these dumb fish are?"

"Maybe they sent out for pizza last night and they're not hungry today," Carole said with a relieved giggle. At least she wouldn't have to kill another worm.

"Well, this day really turned out to be a bust," Colonel Hanson laughed. "First I burn the pancakes, then we capsize the boat, then we fish all day and don't get one bite! Has anything gone right?"

Carole thought for a minute. "Yup," she said. "Two things, in fact."

"Name 'em," her father said.

"One is that we've been sitting together in the sunshine, so our clothes are completely dry."

"That's one."

"And the other is that we've been sitting together in the sunshine."

"That's two," said the colonel, giving his daughter a hug and a kiss.

CAROLE AND HER father lugged the waterlogged canoe back into their campsite just as the sun was beginning to set through the tops of the pine trees.

"I don't know about you, but I feel like I could collapse almost as easily as a collapsible canoe!" Colonel Hanson laughed, but Carole could see beads of perspiration dotting his forehead.

"I know," Carole said. "It was a pretty rough climb. Why don't you relax for a while? It's my turn to cook supper, anyway."

"Okay. Let me charge up the cookstove for you," Colonel Hanson said.

Carole shook her head. "Thanks, Dad, but tonight I just want to build a regular old fire and have regular old hot dogs cooked over it."

"That sounds great, but wouldn't it be easier on the solar stove?"

"Maybe. But I want to try it first this way."

Colonel Hanson laughed. "Okay. You're the chef. I think I'll stretch out in one of the armchairs."

"Fine. Dinner will be ready in no time."

While her father relaxed in the chair, Carole hurried into the woods, gathering the sticks and other tinder she would need to start a fire. She found a dead pine log that was exactly the right size, and in a few minutes she had a cozy campfire going about ten feet from the front of their tent.

"I don't know what you're cooking, but it smells great," her father called with his eyes closed.

"I haven't cooked anything yet, Dad. That's just the wood burning." Carole smiled. Solar cookstoves might be handy, but nothing beat the smell of a real campfire.

She went back into the woods to search for some twigs to roast the hot dogs on. The sticks had to be cut from live bushes, since dead ones would burn up right along with the food. She found a huge forsythia bush and cut four long branches, then peeled the bark back to reveal the milky white layer underneath.

"Perfect," she said aloud. "These will be the best hot dogs Dad ever ate!"

She carried the sticks back to their camp, then loaded two of them with hot dogs and the other two with buns. She placed them just the right distance away from the fire and sat down to watch them cook. Soon her mouth began to water as the smell of grilling hot dogs filled the air. Her favorite outdoor meal was almost done. Suddenly she jumped up. She hadn't gotten anything else together for dinner. She hurried back over and began to set the table as fast as she could. She set out the paper plates, poured a serving of potato chips onto each one, and poured fruit juice into two glasses. What else? She looked at the table. Mustard! Everyone needed mustard with their hot dogs. She ran and opened the solar refrigerator. The mustard was there somewhere—she'd seen it that morning when she was searching for the butter. There, far on the back shelf. Just as she was reaching for it, she smelled an odd, awful smell. *Oh no!* she thought. *The hot dogs are burning!*

She raced back to the fire, where orange flames were licking around the green sticks. The hot dogs had been singed to dark brown, and the buns were just pieces of long toast. She quickly removed all four sticks from the fire, but she wanted to cry. Her wonderful hot dog dinner was ruined.

She carried everything to the table and called her father.

Colonel Hanson had been dozing in his chair, but he rose and came to the table quickly.

"Hey, this looks . . ."

"Burned," Carole said miserably. "Somehow I misjudged the fire. When I was looking for the mustard, everything got burned."

"Oh, hey, it's just a little extra brown," Colonel Hanson said, looking at the charred hot dog on his plate. "That's how I like them, anyway."

Carole knew that her father was only trying to make her feel better. "Use some of this," she said, passing him the mustard. "Maybe it will make it taste better."

Colonel Hanson grinned. "Just like the jam and syrup improved my pancakes?"

"Well, kind of," Carole admitted with a smile.

"Maybe we're not such great outdoor cooks, honey," Colonel Hanson said as he squirted mustard on his hot dog.

"Maybe not," said Carole.

"On the other hand, maybe if you'd used that solar stove, these hot dogs would have turned out perfect!"

"I don't know, Dad. So far the solar stove and the collapsible canoe have given us more headaches than anything else!"

"OKAY, STARLIGHT," STEVIE said with pride. "You are one clean horse." She backed away from the big bay gelding and looked at him approvingly. His coat sparkled like satin, his mane glistened like silk, and his hooves had been polished to a patent-leather sheen.

"I'll say," added Lisa, leaning over the stall door. "How many times have we groomed him today? Four? I know we've gone through three complete changes of clothes."

"Just three times, if you count his shampoo."

"Stevie, I don't think that counts. We got a lot wetter than Starlight did, plus you backed up and fell in a whole tub of water."

"Well, okay. He's had two complete groomings and half a shampoo. Between that and exercising him twice, we've kept our promise to Carole." Stevie handed Starlight's dandy brush to Lisa and backed out of the stall. "I don't know about you, but I'm exhausted."

"Me too. My head is spinning so, I can barely remember what all we've done today."

Stevie picked up Starlight's grooming supplies and walked toward the tack room. "Well, first we mucked out about a million stalls. Then Denise came and we had to help her out at the front desk because she had laryngitis and couldn't talk on the telephone."

"Then we had to tack up Patch for that little girl who'd put his saddle on backwards," Lisa added with a laugh.

"Right. Then we exercised Danny for an hour, since Red didn't have time to do it." Stevie flipped the tack room light on and put Starlight's gear in the proper place. "But thanks to us, Danny's looking great. Veronica should be amazed when she gets back from her shopping trip."

"She won't be, though," said Lisa. "She'll just find something else wrong with him."

"Oh, probably." Stevie turned the light off and closed the door. She rubbed the back of her legs. "Those exercises we did with Starlight today were really hard. I'm sore."

"I know. I had no idea Carole was putting him through such an intense dressage drill."

Stevie laughed. "I had no idea Carole would be putting *us* through such an intense dressage drill."

The girls walked through the empty stable toward the hayloft, their boots echoing in the stillness. They heard an occasional chomping of hay as they passed, and once in a while a horse would pop its head out to see who was going by, but for the most part the stable was getting ready to bed down for the night.

"Don't forget we've got that picnic supper my mom brought us," said Lisa.

"I know," yawned Stevie. "I've been looking forward to it all afternoon.

They paused at Prancer's stall. "Hi, girl," Lisa said softly, leaning over and rubbing the bay mare's neck. "I'm sorry I haven't been able to pay as much attention to you as usual—it's just that I've had to pay so much attention to everybody else!"

Lisa looked at Stevie. "Every time I've gone by here

today, Prancer's just poked her head out of the stall and given me the saddest look!"

"She misses you like Belle misses me. But all this will be over Monday. Then we can take them on a nice ride and give them some extra attention."

Lisa gave Prancer a final pat, and she and Stevie began to head for the hayloft. "Just a minute," Stevie said as they neared Belle's stall. "I want to check that bruise on Belle's shoulder."

Lisa watched as Stevie went inside Belle's stall. The mare flinched when Stevie ran her fingers over the lump at the top of her withers.

"That must still hurt," Stevie said, frowning. "I'd better put some liniment on it tomorrow. That'll make her feel better."

They said good night to Belle, then slowly climbed the ladder. The hayloft looked like a cozy retreat, complete with Mrs. Atwood's picnic basket waiting for them on a bale of hay.

"Arrrggghhh!" Stevie flopped down on her sleeping bag. "I don't think I've ever been this tired before in my entire life."

"Me neither," said Lisa. "Let's just eat something fast and go to sleep."

"Good idea. What did your mom bring?"

Lisa opened the basket and looked inside. "Cold fried chicken, corn chips, carrot sticks, some bottled water, and some little pecan pies."

"Hmmm," said Stevie, extending her arm without moving the rest of her body. "Just put something in this hand and I'll eat it while I doze."

Lisa frowned. "What do you want?"

"Anything," moaned Stevie. "At this point it doesn't matter."

Lisa put a chicken leg in Stevie's hand and grabbed another for herself. In a few minutes most of the chicken was gone, along with the chips and the pecan pie. A few minutes after that, everybody at Pine Hollow, including the guests in the hayloft, was sound asleep and dreaming of the day to come.

8

"THAT WAS A great dinner, Carole." Colonel Hanson stretched in the camping armchair. "The food totally refreshed me, and I don't even feel tired anymore. Must be the magic of home cooking."

"Whatever you say, Dad." Carole smiled. She knew the hot dogs hadn't really tasted that good, but he was nice to say so.

Colonel Hanson looked at her. "Do you still want to go stargazing tonight?"

"Sure," Carole replied eagerly. "I could go stargazing every night. There's so much to see."

"Okay. Let me check my barometer to make sure a front's not coming through." Colonel Hanson dug the little electronic barometer out of his pocket and held it close to the fire. "Everything looks okay," he reported, grinning at Carole. "No bad weather coming, but why don't you grab our jackets while I get the telescope? It gets chilly on top of that mountain."

"Okay." Carole hurried to the tent and got her father's leather flight jacket and the old red quilted coat that she usually wore to the barn.

They doused Carole's small cooking fire with water, and Colonel Hanson hoisted the telescope over his shoulder. Though the path to the top of Mount Stringfellow was somewhat more familiar to them, Carole, leading, shined her flashlight to guide them.

"Gosh, Dad, by the time we get there, the stars will already be out."

"I know. It should be perfect for stargazing." Colonel Hanson looked up at the sky. "Maybe tonight we'll be able to see the Perseid meteor showers."

Carole smiled up at the few dim stars that were already twinkling through the trees. Of all the things they'd done on this trip, looking at the stars was her favorite. Never had the heavens shone more brightly for her and her dad.

By the time they reached the top of Mount Stringfellow, the sky was black velvet spangled with a million diamonds. Over their heads a wide band of even brighter stars stretched across the sky. Carole gasped. "Is that the Milky Way?"

Her father looked up and smiled. "That's what it is. Pretty impressive, huh?"

"It's amazing. I've never seen it so clearly before."

"Well, it's so clear tonight that you can see the whole thing."

Carole stared up at the band of brilliant stars while her father set up the telescope. A brisk breeze skimmed the top of the mountain, and both of them slipped into their jackets.

"Okay," her father called, his head bent over the eyepiece. "Here's our old pal Saturn, still surrounded by rings." He stood up straight and looked at Carole. "Want to come have a look?"

"Sure." She hurried over to the telescope. Saturn looked just as beautiful as it had the night before— an icy yellow ball suspended in a black sky. The rings looked like giant flat roads racing around the planet.

"Let's see if we can find Mars next," her father suggested.

They found the red planet and tried to count the canals, then tried to focus on Venus—but the stars suddenly seemed to glow less brightly. When her father began to search for Mercury, Carole began to yawn. As wonderful as looking at the stars was, she felt as if she'd been up forever.

"Hey, Dad, I think I'm going to lie down while you look for Mercury," she said, snuggling down on the ground in her quilted jacket.

Colonel Hanson smiled. "Take a snooze if you want

to. I'll wake you up when I find something spectacular."

"Thanks." She folded her arms behind her head, but not before she felt a funny lump in the left pocket of her jacket. She reached inside it and smiled—she'd left one of Starlight's leg wraps coiled up in a soft ball. She'd have to remember to put it in her cubby when they got back to civilization.

Starlight. Her horse's name suddenly had a whole new meaning. It was as if she'd never known what starlight was until this trip. Her mind wandered back to Pine Hollow, and she thought about her friends and the fun they must be having. Were they looking after her horse as they'd promised? Of course. That was what friends did. This weekend it was as if Starlight had two owners instead of one. He was a lucky horse indeed.

Carole settled back down and looked up into the Milky Way, thoughts of Pine Hollow settling comfortably into the back of her mind.

Though the stars twinkled a little more dimly than they had earlier, it was still the most magical and mysterious thing she'd ever seen. She sighed and felt like a tiny spot in the universe, no bigger than the amoebas she'd studied in science the previous year. She felt her eyelids growing heavy as she thought about amoebas and stars and starlight and Starlight and Stevie and Lisa and—

Carole jumped. A loud rumble had broken the stillness of the night. Something must have fallen nearby. Maybe it was the telescope! She opened her eyes. She was still lying on the top of Mount Stringfellow; in fact, her father was curled up just a short distance away. He must have gotten as tired as she had and fallen asleep, too. But what was that noise she'd heard?

She rose on one elbow. A fierce gust of wind blew hard against her eyes and she felt the sting of raindrops on her face. She tried to look up at the stars, but they were gone, covered by a huge black storm cloud that blotted all light from the sky.

"Dad!" she cried. "Dad! We need to get out of here!"

"What?" Colonel Hanson jolted awake.

"A storm has blown up. We need to find some shelter." The wind suddenly started to blow so hard that Carole had to yell to be heard. She watched her father get up and grab the telescope.

"Let's go over to those rocks!" he yelled, pointing to a pile of boulders on the very top of the mountain. "We'll be safe there as long as there's no lightning!"

He grabbed her by the hand and pulled her to her feet, and together they ran toward the boulders. They hadn't taken three steps before rain began to pour down so hard that Carole had trouble keeping her eyes open. It was impossible to see anything, and the wind howled like some savage animal. It whipped the rain against her even harder. She lowered her head and ran hard to keep up with her father.

Finally they reached the boulders. There was a small outcropping of rock that sheltered them from the rain, but not the wind. "Are you okay?" her father yelled, frowning with concern.

Carole nodded. "I just hope it doesn't start lightening."

"If we're lucky, it won't," Colonel Hanson said just as a huge clap of thunder broke overhead. He turned to scan the northwest horizon. As he did, blistering fingers of lightning crackled down from the clouds. First one, then another, and a third. All reaching from the heart of a dark black cloud down to the earth below; all seemed to be heading straight toward Carole and her father.

"Did you see that?" her father shouted as another clap of thunder rent the air.

Carole nodded; she was too scared to speak.

Colonel Hanson looked at her gravely. "We've got to get off this mountain now! That storm's tracking straight at us, and this is the absolute worst place to be in a thunderstorm."

"Where can we go?" she asked in a squeaky voice.

"We'd be better off under a lot of trees in a valley,

but anyplace is better than this," her father yelled. "Grab your flashlight and we'll try to find the trail back down the mountain!"

"Okay." Fortunately, Carole had remembered to pick up her flashlight when the storm had started. She switched it on, but its normally bright beam looked more like a candle in the thick, wet darkness.

"Hurry!" Her father yelled. "And stay close behind me!"

They scurried away from the shelter of the rocks, the raindrops once again stinging them like needles. The wind almost toppled them, and they had to bend forward at the waist to get anywhere at all.

Carole followed her father blindly, trailing after his dark shape as he pushed his way through the wind and rain. The thunder crashed directly over them, and just a few hundred yards away, Carole saw a bolt of bright lightning streak down from the sky. It crackled around the top of one tall pine, and the highest tree limbs exploded like a bomb. Carole could make out the dark outline of birds fleeing the sudden inferno.

"Keep your head down!" her father called. "I think the trail's over here!"

Shaking with fear, she followed him to the edge of some scraggly trees. Underbrush tugged at their jeans as they tried to press themselves beneath the branches. Abruptly her father stopped.

"Wait." He turned and tried to peer through the

rain at where they'd just been. Carole turned and looked too, but her flashlight was useless and she could see clearly only when the lightning flashed. Unfortunately, that was when it was hardest to keep her eyes open.

"Oh, no!" she heard her father cry.

"What?" She was barely able to make herself heard above the wind and rain.

"We must have gotten disoriented when we got up so fast," he called, his voice now hoarse from yelling. "The trail's over there, right across from where we just were."

Carole's heart skittered with fear. "You mean we're going to have to cross the mountaintop again?"

Her father nodded as raindrops dripped off his chin. "These trees won't be safe if that storm stays on track." He looked down at her and grinned. "Are you with me, kiddo?" he asked softly.

Again, she only nodded. She was afraid that if she spoke out loud he'd know how scared she was.

"Okay, then, let's go!" He shifted the telescope to his other shoulder and gave her a thumbs-up. *"Semper fi!"*

Colonel Hanson waited until a clap of thunder rolled away, then stepped out from the shelter of the skinny trees. Again they had to bend at the waist and throw themselves into the wind. The rain seem to hit them from all directions, and Carole felt icy raindrops sliding down her back, under the collar of her jacket. Everything she had on was soaked, and her feet slid inside her shoes. Still, she slogged after her father.

They had almost reached the middle of the mountaintop when suddenly the sky lit up as if a million fireworks had all exploded. A crash of thunder like no other boomed around Carole's ears. The earth itself seemed to tremble beneath her feet. The sky went bright, then dark; then she couldn't see anything. Where was her father? He had been there just a moment before. The sky lit up again, and she saw his crumpled form.

"Dad!" she screamed, just as another thunderclap crashed above her head.

9

"YEOW!" LISA SAT straight up in her sleeping bag, her heart thumping in her chest. "What was that?"

"I think it was a horse." Stevie blinked sleepily, but she was already sitting up. "Something's wrong downstairs. We'd better go check it out."

They switched on the hayloft light and began to crawl down the ladder. Suddenly a loud boom shook the roof overhead; then the shrill scream of a horse split the air.

"That's what woke me up!" cried Lisa.

"I bet it's Patch," said Stevie as rain began to ping like marbles against the barn's tin roof. "You know how crazy he gets when we have thunderstorms."

The two girls hurried down to Patch's stall. Sure enough, the old pinto stood there terrified, his ears slapped flat against his head, the whites of his eyes showing all around.

"Whoa, boy," Stevie said softly, reaching out and trying to pat the horse's nose. "Take it easy." Patch swished his tail and stomped his right foreleg. Stevie wanted to go into the stall and put her arms around him, but he looked so terrified that it was safer to stay outside.

Another thunderclap rattled the barn, and Patch seemed to jump a foot into the air.

"He looks upset enough to hurt himself," said Lisa. "What should we do?"

Stevie frowned. "Max usually gives him a tranquilizer when bad weather's on the way, but this storm sneaked up on us. I guess we could give him one of his pills and stay with him until it takes effect."

Lisa reached over and rubbed Patch's soft nose. "Too bad we don't have any equine earplugs."

"Wait a minute!" Stevie snapped her fingers. "You just gave me a fantastic idea. Stay right here!"

Lisa watched as Stevie ran back to the ladder that led to the hayloft. She scurried up, and in just a moment she came back down, clutching her CD player in one hand.

"Stevie, what are you going to do?" Lisa asked as Stevie ran back down the aisle.

Stevie looked at her and grinned. "Earplugs blot out unwanted noise, right?"

Lisa nodded.

"Well, so does other, louder, constant noise." Stevie held up her CD player. "If I play my new CD over the PA system, the horses won't be able to hear the thunderstorm so much. This music will lull them back to sleep, just like babies!"

"But Stevie, you played me that CD last night—it's all screaming guitars and thumping drums and weird synthesizers. It would be more likely to wake the dead than lull anything to sleep."

"I'll bet it works, though. I'm going to go hook this up. I bet we'll have a barnful of drowsy horses in no time!"

"I think I'll give poor Patch his tranquilizer, anyway," said Lisa. "He looks like he's about to have a nervous breakdown."

As she was getting one of Patch's blue capsules and an apple, all sorts of strange, electronic noises started chirping from the speakers overhead. When she walked back to Patch's stall, she noticed that all the horses that had been sound asleep were now standing at their stall doors, their ears flicking at the electric guitar music that was bouncing around the ceiling.

"Okay, Patch," Lisa said as she reached the distraught horse. "Just a few more minutes and you'll feel fine." She cut the apple in two, then opened the capsule and poured tiny grains of yellow medicine across the fleshy part of the fruit.

"Here, boy," she said, holding one half out to Patch. "Eat this." As terrified as Patch was, he still couldn't resist nibbling an apple. In just a second, he'd swallowed the half with a satisfied crunch.

Lisa held the rest of it out. Patch was just as excited about the second half as he'd been about the first. He was chomping happily away when someone started singing over the PA system.

"You've got to know-ow-ow-ow-ow," a high-pitched singer yowled, *"The best time to go-o-o-o . . ."*

Lisa looked at Patch, expecting him to jump straight into the air. Instead he just stood there, once again the calm horse she'd always known him to be.

"Well, Patch, maybe Stevie's on to something," Lisa said, again rubbing his nose. "I know your medicine couldn't have worked that fast."

Just then she heard a bump in the neighboring stall. She left Patch and peaked inside. Prancer had woken up and was anxiously looking out her stall door.

"Hey, girl," Lisa said as Stevie's music shrieked even more loudly. She had just begun to scratch her favorite horse behind the ears when she heard a high-pitched whinny of panic from the far end of the stable.

"Oh no!" she said, giving Prancer a last pat. "That's Starlight! Sorry, girl. I'll be right back!"

She ran down to Starlight's stall. He stood just as Patch had a few moments earlier, with his ears slapped back and his nostrils flaring wide, showing the pink insides of his nose. He paced back and forth in his stall.

"Uh-oh," said Lisa, reaching out to give him a reassuring touch.

"Hi!" Stevie suddenly turned the corner. "How's it working? Is everybody back to sleep yet?"

"Well, Patch is fine, but now Starlight looks wired." Lisa frowned as the big bay stomped his foot. "I think he might be more of a Mozart horse, Stevie. Heavy metal doesn't seem to be doing a thing for him."

"Hang on." Stevie went to the hayloft ladder and scampered up. A few moments later she came back down with an extra red sweater she'd brought in case they got cold.

"I'll tie this over his ears," she said, letting herself into Starlight's stall. "That should fix everything so it won't be quite so loud."

At first Starlight tossed his head at Stevie's sweater, but he finally stood still while she positioned it over his ears and tied it under his chin.

"There!" she said, stepping back to admire her work. "What do you think?"

Lisa laughed at the sight. "He looks like someone's grandmother, Stevie," she giggled. "I'm glad Carole's not here to see her horse wrapped in a babushka."

Stevie shrugged. "She probably would think it was strange, but it seems to work. He's calmer."

"Maybe we should go see how everybody else is doing, since we're already up," Lisa suggested.

"Good idea," agreed Stevie.

They started walking all around the big U of the stable. Most of the horses had gotten used to the guitars shrieking through the barn and had settled back down to go to sleep. Though Stevie's music drowned out a lot of the thunder, the girls could still hear the rain beating down on the roof.

"I wonder if the roof has any leaks," Stevie said, peering into Doc's stall.

"Yes," answered Lisa as she checked on Danny.

"How do you know?" said Stevie.

"Because Danny's standing here in a big puddle."

"Uh-oh." Stevie frowned. "That won't be good for his leg. We'd better get him out of there, and fast."

Lisa ran to the tack room and got two cross-ties while Stevie put Danny's halter on him and led him to the center of the aisle. Danny didn't look as nervous about the music as he looked miserable from standing in a wet stall.

"Let's get a rag and dry him off," said Stevie as Lisa cross-tied him. "Then we'd better change his leg wrap."

"Poor baby," said Lisa. "He's worked so hard to get well, and now he's stuck in a leaky stall."

Lisa dried Danny with a towel while Stevie found a clean leg wrap to replace the wet one. Just as she was tying off one end, a heavy thunk came from the other side of the stable.

"Now what?" said Lisa. "I can barely catch my breath from one thing when something else goes wrong."

"I don't know. You go and see while I finish up here."

Lisa left Stevie with Danny and hurried over to investigate. The thunk sounded as if it had come from Max's office. Slowly Lisa cracked open the door and turned on the light.

"Oh no!" she cried. Someone had left the window open, and the wind had blown Max's big bookcase over. About fifty horse books were scattered on the floor, wet from the rain blowing in the window.

"Gosh," Lisa said, hurrying across the room and pulling the window shut. "I wonder what else could possibly go wrong tonight?"

She pushed the bookcase back against the wall and spread the books out on Max's desk. They would have to dry before they could be reshelved. She and Stevie could take care of that in the morning.

She turned off the light, closed the door, and hurried back down the aisle. Stevie had just finished drying Danny off, and he looked clean and neat once again.

"That's one lucky horse to have us taking care of him," said Lisa, admiring Stevie's leg wrap.

"Oh, it just makes up for the bad luck of being owned by Veronica," Stevie muttered. "She probably would have just left him standing in a wet stall all night."

Suddenly Lisa cocked her head to one side. "Do you hear that?"

"Yeah. It's my favorite song on this whole album."

"No, not the song. That other, fainter sound. That weird *scree, slam; scree, slam*."

Stevie turned her head and listened. "Yeah, I do. Wonder what it is? It doesn't sound like a horse."

"It doesn't sound like a bookcase falling over, either." Lisa frowned. "Do you think it could be one of those spooky noises Max warned us about?"

"I don't know. Let's turn the music down a little and see where it's coming from."

They went to the office and turned down the PA system, then made a two-person patrol of the stable. Most of the horses were asleep again, and the girls felt as if they were suddenly all alone. *Scree, slam; scree, slam*. The eerie noise continued, now louder and echoing through the barn.

"Do you think it could be a ghost?" said Stevie as they came to a dark part of the stable where the overhead light had burned out.

Lisa felt the gooseflesh rise on her arms. "I don't think so." She looked up at the shadowy ceiling. "But I sure wish there was a light up there."

100

"Remind me to change that lightbulb in the morning," said Stevie in a whisper.

"Why are you whispering?" whispered Lisa.

"I don't know. Probably the same reason you're walking on tiptoe."

Slowly the girls crept forward. *Scree, slam! Scree, slam!* The noise grew louder. Nothing they'd ever heard in a stable made a noise like that. Stevie was just about to grab Lisa's hand and run back to the bright end of the stable when Lisa stopped.

"Stevie, look!" She pointed to the last stall in the row—a big empty one that Max occasionally used for a foaling stall. The shutter had not been latched securely, and every time the wind gusted, it blew out with a *scree* and swung shut with a *slam*. "There's our ghost," Lisa said with a laugh. "An unlatched shutter!"

"I knew it all along," said Stevie as she stepped into the stall and closed the shutter tight.

"Yeah, right, Stevie." Lisa rolled her eyes.

"The rain seems to be letting up," Stevie said, drying her hands on her pants. "Let's go turn the music off and see if we can dry out Danny's stall. Then maybe we can go back to bed and get some rest ourselves."

They went back to the office and turned off the PA system. The stable now echoed with an odd, empty silence, but the horses didn't seem to mind. Most were already either stretched out in their straw or dozing on their feet as Lisa and Stevie hurried back to Danny.

"I'll muck out Danny's stall if you'll go get some dry straw for him to sleep on," Stevie offered.

"Okay," Lisa agreed.

Stevie forked up Danny's wet straw while Lisa filled the big wheelbarrow. Because they worked together the job went quickly, and soon Danny was standing in a nice dry stall full of fresh straw. He gave a big sigh as Lisa and Stevie latched the door behind him.

"Sounds like he's glad to get back to bed," Lisa laughed.

"I will be, too," yawned Stevie. "Do you know what time it is?"

Lisa shook her head.

"Well, we've got about an hour before the first riders start knocking on our door."

"You're kidding!" Lisa's blue eyes looked red and tired. "That storm took most of the night?"

"The storm, plus Patch, plus Starlight, plus Danny . . . ," Stevie rattled off.

"Okay, okay," Lisa said. "Let's just hurry so we can at least get a nap before everybody starts arriving."

They turned off the barn lights, but not before Stevie had untied Starlight's babushka hat and let the big bay fall asleep without any headgear on.

"Did you ever get a chance to check on Belle?" Lisa asked as she trudged up the ladder.

"No. Did you check on Prancer?"

"Only for about five seconds," Lisa yawned. "I will first thing in the morning, though."

"You mean first thing in about forty-five minutes," Stevie said as she fell into her sleeping bag.

"Right," answered Lisa. She collapsed just the way Stevie had, then suddenly sat up. "Is your sleeping bag wet?" she asked.

"Yuccch," Stevie replied, feeling the damp material with both hands. "It is."

"Oh, no. Look." Lisa pointed at the roof above their heads, where a rosy sliver of light was peeking through. "Guess who else had a leak in the roof of their stalls?"

"*Arrggghhhh*," Stevie cried as she rolled up in a dry blanket and closed her eyes, desperate to at least get twenty minutes of sleep before the next long day began.

10

"DAD! ARE YOU okay?" Carole could barely make out her father's form.

"Yes, I just slipped and fell." Her father turned and squinted at her through the driving rain. "Could you give me a hand?"

"Sure." She hurried over to where he lay, her feet slurping through the slick mud. She held out her right hand and then, when he grabbed it, pulled back. He rose to his feet slowly, still carefully holding the telescope on his shoulder.

"Are you sure you're all right?" she asked again, raising her voice to be heard over the pounding rain.

"For somebody carrying a big metal telescope across the top of a mountain in an electrical storm, I'm do-

104

ing as well as can be expected," he said with a small laugh.

Carole felt better immediately. As long as her father was still cracking jokes, everything was okay.

"Let's see if we can find our trail again," he called, shielding his eyes against the rain. "I think it's over that way."

"Okay, but let's go more slowly so nobody will fall," Carole called back.

Her father signaled another thumbs-up and began to pick his way carefully across the muddy mountaintop. Carole followed a few feet behind him. The rain was not falling as hard now, or as fast. Nor was the lightning so close. A strike of light and three seconds of silence before the rumble of thunder suggested that the storm was moving on. If they could just find their trail through the woods, they would be out of it altogether.

Suddenly she saw her father raise one arm and motion her forward. *He's found the path*, she thought. She walked as quickly as she dared behind him. A second later she could see the tall shapes of trees all around them. They had made it! They had escaped Mount Stringfellow!

"Let's hurry on to camp now," her father called. "The wind's blowing the storm away, but the lightning will probably hang around for a while. Just follow me!"

"Okay," Carole replied.

She watched as her father scrambled down the path they'd climbed up so many hours before. His dark leather jacket blended in with the trees, but the white telescope bouncing on his shoulder acted like an arrow, pointing the way back to camp. She followed him past some familiar logs, then past a huge pine tree, then over a rocky place in the trail. She saw the telescope bob around the edge of a small clearing; then she stopped.

Suddenly she felt funny. Her heart began to beat faster. A strange, high-pitched whine hummed through the air, and she felt as if someone were trying to pull her into the sky by her hair.

"Dad!" she started to cry, but her throat seemed to close up around her words. An eerie blue light lit the clearing and her cheeks began to sting as if someone had slapped her. Her whole body started shaking, and she closed her eyes. A noise like a jet engine slammed into the ground behind her, shuddering the earth beneath her feet. Her brain seemed to spin. *What's going on?* she wanted to cry. *A plane crash? An earthquake?* She felt weak all over, but she managed to open her eyes. To her horror, her father had disappeared again.

"Dad?" It took all her strength to speak, and her voice sounded funny and far away. She shook her head, then tried to hurry on through the clearing, her legs tingling all the way down to her toes.

"Carole!" she heard a faint voice calling. "Carole! Are you all right?"

"I'm here, Dad." She tried to see into the darkness. "Where are you?"

"Over here!"

She squinted. There, beneath a large oak tree, she saw the skinny white shape of the telescope. She hurried over. Her father lay on the ground beside it, his face etched with pain.

"What happened?" she gasped, gratefully sliding down in the mud beside him.

"Lightning struck right behind you! I turned around to run back to help you and tripped over that root." Colonel Hanson winced. "Are you okay?"

"I think so," she said, her words still coming out slowly. "How about you?"

"I think I've sprained my ankle."

She looked at his ankle. It was lying at an odd angle to the rest of his leg, looking far worse than sprained. "Oh, Dad," she cried. "I think it might be broken."

"No, it's not broken," Colonel Hanson said, out of breath. "Let's just sit here a minute and think about how we can get out of this mess. Are you sure you're all right?"

"I don't know," Carole said woozily. "I feel strange." Her heart was still beating rapidly, and her palms were clammy. *So that's what almost being struck by lightning is like*, she thought. *Wow. I must be really lucky.* She sat still for a long moment, letting the now gentle rain cool her hot face. After she'd taken a few deep breaths, her head seemed to clear and she felt more like her old self. *Okay*, she thought. *We're in trouble and I've got to help out. How?* She stuffed her cold hands in her jacket pockets. Then she smiled as her fingers touched Starlight's leg wrap. If she could bandage her father's ankle with it, he might be able to hobble back to camp.

"Okay, Dad," she said, turning to him. "Let's see what that ankle really looks like. Hold the flashlight."

Colonel Hanson held the flashlight while Carole unlaced his boot. She pulled it off as gently as she could, but he grimaced with every move she made.

"Ouch!" he yelped as she pulled off his sock.

His ankle was badly swollen. "It's a good thing you took that boot off when you did," he said. "Otherwise we'd have had to cut it off, and I'd be out one good camping boot." He looked at her. "What are you going to do now, Dr. Hanson?"

"Well, I'm going to use Starlight's leg wrap like an Ace bandage," Carole said, gently lifting the stretchy cotton around her dad's foot and crisscrossing it over his ankle. "We learned how to do this in health class last year."

"And?"

108

Carole smiled. "And then I'm hoping you'll be able to walk back to camp, using me as a crutch."

She tied the leg wrap as snugly as she could for support, then helped her father to his feet. The rain and lightning had stopped completely, and once again the stars shone brightly above Mount Stringfellow. "Want to try a few steps?" she said, positioning herself under his left shoulder.

"Okay," he groaned. He hopped forward on one foot, but Carole was not tall enough to support him. "I don't think this is going to work," he whispered painfully, and she helped him sit back down.

"Okay," he said, trying to keep his voice light. "Got any ideas for Plan B? Your old dad seems to be coming up dry."

"I could go back down to the car and call the park ranger from the cell phone," Carole said.

"That might be the best idea, honey," Colonel Hanson said. "They're trained to do these sorts of rescues. But are you sure you're up for a long hike at night, all by yourself? It's over a mile back to the car. Won't you be afraid?"

Carole shook her head. "Not nearly as afraid now that I've nearly been struck by lightning," she said with a laugh.

"I guess lightning does sort of put things in perspective," her father said, chuckling. "Are you sure you know the way back?"

"I'll just stay on this trail," she said. "Now that the stars are back out, it's actually pretty easy to see." She leaned over and gave her father a hug. "You stay still. I'll be back as soon as I can."

"Yes ma'am, Dr. Hanson." Her father gave her a sitting salute. "You be careful yourself."

"Don't worry." Carole smiled, turned, picked up the telescope, and hurried away into the night.

Fortunately, the camp was not too far away. Carole walked quickly along the trail, her boots squishing through the wet grass. Raindrops still dripped from the leaves of the trees, and every now and then she would hear a strange chirp or whistle in the forest. *I could get real scared if I let myself*, she thought. *Right now I'll just concentrate on getting back to the car safely.*

She kept walking, confidently putting one foot in front of the other until finally, glowing dully through the trees, she saw the big orange mushroom that was their tent. She let out a deep breath. As goofy as that tent looked in the daytime, it sure looked good right then.

She hurried back to the orange lump. Their old fire was a soggy circle of ashes, but the tent and all their supplies were in good shape. She went inside, placed the telescope in a corner, and turned on the solar lantern. Its warm glow made their sleeping bags seem as inviting as their own beds at home.

"Maybe some of this solar stuff isn't such a bad

idea," she whispered. She dried her face and began searching for her dad's car keys. He usually kept them in his toiletry kit, but they weren't there. She did find the electronic barometer, which still indicated clear skies and low pressure. Carole shook her head ruefully. Obviously it was broken. She tossed it aside and continued searching for the keys. She was just beginning to search through the pockets of his jeans when she heard a familiar sound.

"Oh, please!" she cried, dropping everything and hurrying to the tent flap. She peeked out. There, just as it had the night before, stood the roan Appaloosa.

"Oh, Rambler!" she cried, giving him her own private name. "Am I glad to see you!"

The horse whinnied and pricked his ears. Carole hurried back outside to find the twine she'd used the night before. It was on top of the solar refrigerator, just where she'd left it.

"Rambler, how would you like to go on a rescue mission?" she asked excitedly, tying the twine to his halter again. This time she looped it around his neck like reins.

Rambler didn't seem to mind, so she grabbed a handful of his mane and hopped up on his back.

"Okay, boy," she said, guiding him with her knees and the makeshift reins. "We're going halfway up Mount Stringfellow."

Rambler responded to her commands eagerly, and

soon they were picking their way along the wet forest trail. Even though Carole could barely see through the thick trees, she knew Rambler could find the best path easily. Rain still dripped on them, and once they slipped in some mud, but together they made much faster progress than she would have alone.

In a few minutes a dim figure appeared underneath some trees to her left.

"Dad?" she called.

"Carole, I'm so glad you came back," he replied. "I just found my car keys."

"I ran into a little help," she said with a giggle, pulling Rambler to a stop in front of her father. She slid off and patted his neck. "Dad, meet Rambler, the horse from next door."

Colonel Hanson's jaw dropped in astonishment. "Is this the one who visited you last night?"

"He's the one," Carole said. "I told him he was going on a rescue mission tonight, and he seemed okay with it."

Colonel Hanson frowned. "How about his owners?"

"Well, let's just say what they don't know won't hurt them."

Carole helped her father struggle to his feet and supported him while he hobbled to Rambler's side.

"How am I going to get on with a sprained ankle?" Colonel Hanson wondered aloud.

"Just bend your left leg and I'll give you an alley-oop. Push off my hand with your knee and your ankle won't be involved at all."

"You horsepeople," Colonel Hanson said, chuckling. "You've got a remedy for everything."

He grabbed Rambler's mane and bent his left leg as Carole had told him. On the count of three she boosted him up, and a second later he was sitting easily on Rambler's bare back.

"Okay," said Carole, leading Rambler by the rope. "Just hang on and we'll be home in no time."

She led the horse slowly back down the trail. He seemed to sense the vulnerability of his rider and softened the jigging gait he'd used with Carole to a smooth, ground-covering walk. In just a little while, the orange tent again beckoned through the trees.

"Wow," said Colonel Hanson. "That tent sure looks good."

"I left the solar light on to welcome us home," said Carole. She led Rambler as close to the tent as she could, then told her dad to keep his left leg bent when he slid off the horse.

"There," said Colonel Hanson as he hit the ground with a soft thud. He hopped on one foot and gave Rambler a good scratch behind the ears. "Thanks, boy," he said. "We're lucky you came visiting again."

"Let's get you in bed," said Carole. She helped her

father hop into the tent and into his sleeping bag. She filled an ice pack from the refrigerator and put it on his ankle.

"I think that's all we can do tonight," she said, looking at the swollen mass of her father's foot.

"I think that's all we can do until we go home," said Colonel Hanson. "If it's broken they won't set it till the swelling goes down. And if it's not broken, just keeping it iced is the best thing we can do right now." He leaned back in his sleeping bag and smiled at Carole.

"Thanks, honey. I'm so proud of you. We were in a real jam up there, and you never lost your head."

"Well, I almost did when the lightning struck," Carole laughed.

"You know what I mean." Her father grinned. "You're a real trouper." He held his hand up. "*Semper fi.*"

"*Semper fi,* Dad," she said, giving him a soft high five. "Right now I think I'd better see that Rambler gets back to his own corral."

"I wish I could help you," Colonel Hanson said.

"Just stay there and rest." Carole smiled. "I'll be back in a few minutes."

When she came through the tent flaps, Rambler hadn't moved.

"Hey, boy," she said softly, grabbing his makeshift reins and leading him to their cooking supplies. "Let's see if there's anything in here you might like. I think you've earned a reward."

She opened the refrigerator and found some apples in the crisper. She took one and fed it to the horse. He chewed noisily and shook his head up and down. Like most horses, apples seemed to be among his favorite treats.

"Thanks for helping me get my dad down from the mountain, boy." She rubbed his soft neck. "You're a champ of a horse. I wish I could keep you, but I've got to take you home."

She hoisted herself onto his back and pointed him in the direction of his campsite. He had no problem navigating through the dark woods, and in just a few minutes he was back in his paddock, nuzzling with his leopard Appaloosa friend. Carole untied the rope from his halter and again secured the loose paddock rope to the tree. "Your owners may be great riders, but they're not such hot paddock makers," Carole whispered, casting a glance at the dark green tent. Obviously the Loftins had tied their tent flaps down against the rain and had slept through the monstrous thunderstorm. Well, she wasn't going to wake them up now to tell them some wild tale about her horse rescuing her father from the mountain. She gave Rambler and his friend a final rub. "You guys be good, now. And stay inside the paddock!"

She turned on her flashlight and hurried back up the trail. They were great horses. She had a feeling they might be wasted on their owners.

By the time she got back to the tent, her father was dozing. His ankle was still elevated on the ice pack, and he seemed to be resting comfortably. *That's great*, she thought as she took her wet jacket off and climbed into her sleeping bag. *A good night's rest will do us both a world of good.* She stayed awake long enough to turn off the solar lamp. A moment later she closed her eyes and fell into a deep, exhausted sleep.

"UGGHHH," LISA GROANED as she smoothed a saddle blanket on Calypso's back. "I can't believe all these people are here to ride this morning. I can barely keep my eyes open."

"Me neither," said Stevie, who was brushing Patch in the next stall. "And all these riders look so bright-eyed and cheerful."

"Right," agreed Lisa. "They act like *they've* had a whole night's sleep! How's Patch this morning?"

"Steady as ever," Stevie reported. "You'd never know there'd been a storm by looking at him. No after–rock band distress, either."

"That's good." Lisa ran Calypso's stirrups up. "At least he won't be jittery when he gets ridden today."

She frowned suddenly. "Stevie, I've been thinking about that storm."

"And?"

"And I think whatever weather system came here would've come through the mountains first. Carole must have been out in the middle of all that thunder and lightning last night."

"Gosh," said Stevie, her hazel eyes clouding with concern. "I hadn't thought of that. But she's with her dad. He's a colonel in the Marine Corps, for Pete's sake."

"I know. But you never know what might happen. Let's take extra-special care of Starlight today, just for Carole."

"Okay," said Stevie, fighting back another yawn. "That way we'll keep ourselves busy and not worry so much, plus we'll be doing exactly what we promised Carole we'd do!"

"RUN, DAD, RUN!" Carole cried. "We need water! We're going to die of thirst!"

"Carole!" Colonel Hanson's voice rang out. "Carole!"

"Huh?" Carole opened her eyes and blinked. She was surrounded on all sides by brilliant orange light. She sat up in her sleeping bag, perspiration dripping from her forehead.

Colonel Hanson laughed. "Wake up, honey. You were having a dream."

Carole looked over at her father. "I dreamed we were in the desert, dying of thirst," she said sheepishly.

"Well, it's hot enough in this tent to feel like the desert." Colonel Hanson sat up and checked his watch. "Good grief! No wonder it's hot. It's almost noon!"

"Wow." Carole rubbed her eyes. "I guess we really slept in." She looked over at her father's leg. He'd slept with it propped up on two pillows, but the ice pack had fallen off in the night. "How does your ankle feel?"

Colonel Hanson moved it slightly, then grimaced with pain. "It's not as swollen as it was last night, but it sure does hurt when I wiggle it."

"If you can move it, then it probably isn't broken," Carole said, slipping out of her sleeping bag. "I guess the horse bandage and the ice were the right things to do."

"I don't think I could have found a better paramedic than you," Colonel Hanson said. "I mean, curb service on horseback in the middle of the night after a thunderstorm?"

Carole giggled. "It was a pretty strange night." She remembered her near miss with the lightning bolt. "Not one I'd like to repeat anytime soon."

119

"How about we just kick back here today?" her father suggested. "I mean, there's no point in cutting our trip short now, since we'll be leaving tomorrow morning anyway. Let's relax and enjoy the rest of our wilderness weekend."

"Fine by me, if you're sure you feel like it," said Carole.

"Just set up one of those folding chairs with a stool close to the fire so I can issue orders to you all day long and I'll be fine," her dad said with a grin.

Carole opened the tent flaps and pulled one of the collapsible armchairs into the bright sunlight. She helped her father to his feet, and together they hobbled to the chair.

"Ah," said Colonel Hanson as Carole elevated his leg with a camping stool. "This is the life."

The day was sunny. High white clouds drifted across a bright blue sky, leaving no hint that the night before had been split by rumbling thunder and crackles of lightning. Carole smiled as she took a deep breath and inhaled the fresh aroma of the pine trees that surrounded them.

"How about I cook us some breakfast?" she said, suddenly aware of her growling stomach.

"Honey, I'll eat whatever you can come up with," her father replied.

She went over and looked in the refrigerator. The chicken was all gone. Other than some fancy freeze-

120

dried dishes that she would have to cook on the solar stove, mostly what they had left was hot dogs. "Do hot dogs sound good?" she called over her shoulder.

"Great!" said her dad.

She cleared out the soggy ashes from the old fire and found enough dry wood in the forest to start another small blaze. She cut several more branches from another forsythia bush, and soon four hot dogs were sizzling over the crackling flames. When they were ready, she fixed two on a paper plate for her dad.

"Mmmmm, this is perfect." Colonel Hanson took a bite of hot dog. "I think you may be right, Carole. Hot dogs over an open fire might just be the best camp meal ever."

"I'm glad you like them, Dad." Carole laughed. "I think we may be having quite a few more."

After breakfast Carole threw another log on the fire and got the tree identification book she'd packed.

"Let's see how many different trees we can find from this one spot," she said, carrying the book over to her dad. "I'll write them down. Who knows, maybe they'll come in handy in school this year." She gave a little shudder at the thought of school. Stevie was right—it did seem incredible that in just three short days she would again be sitting at a desk, working on book reports and science projects.

"Okay." Colonel Hanson flipped to the section on conifers and pointed to a huge pine tree directly in front of them. "I bet that big tree there is a loblolly pine."

"Look it up and see if you're right." Carole leaned over his shoulder.

What Colonel Hanson thought was a loblolly pine turned out to be an eastern hemlock, but soon they had correctly identified all the trees that surrounded their campsite.

"That's amazing, isn't it?" Colonel Hanson said. "I would have said there were two or three different species, and we've named almost twenty."

"It is pretty amazing," replied Carole. "I wonder how many birds we could see from this one spot?"

Colonel Hanson smiled. "Get your bird book out and we'll give it a try."

Carole exchanged her tree book for her bird book. In just a little while, she and her father had found chickadees, grosbeaks, and a beautiful bright-colored bird called a scarlet tanager.

"Gosh," said Carole, looking through the telescope. "This is really neat. There are almost as many birds as there are trees."

"It's too bad we don't take more time to really look at them at home," Colonel Hanson said.

They found a pileated woodpecker and an ovenbird. Then Carole cooked more hot dogs. After they ate they relaxed by the fire with other books they'd brought from home. Carole had the new horse book

122

she'd wanted to read, but it was hard to pay attention to it and not think of Stevie and Lisa and Starlight. She couldn't help wondering if their Pine Hollow sleepover had been as exciting as her campout in the forest. She smiled. She didn't imagine they'd almost been struck by lightning, but anything Stevie was involved with was likely to have a lot of fireworks!

Slowly the sun slipped downward in the sky. When the clouds behind the eastern hemlocks grew pink, Carole put her book aside.

"Are you ready for some supper?" she asked her dad.

"Anytime you are, honey," Colonel Hanson replied. "What's for dinner?"

She grinned, embarrassed. "Since we had hot dogs *en brochette* for breakfast and hot dogs flambés for lunch, how about hot dogs *à la Carole* for dinner?"

"I was hoping we'd have that." Colonel Hanson laughed. "Tell me, what do hot dogs *à la Carole* taste like?"

Carole sighed. "Actually, they taste a lot like hot dogs *en brochette* and hot dogs flambés."

"Fine with me," Colonel Hanson said, still smiling.

Carole built the fire up and found some more green sticks for the hot dogs. By the time she had everything ready to cook, the sun had gone down and the fire was a cozy circle of warmth in a cool evening.

"These are great, honey," Colonel Hanson said, his

mouth full. "I think hot dogs *à la Carole* are my favorite."

"Thanks, Dad," she giggled, dousing her bun with mustard and ketchup.

They finished their supper and relaxed beside the fire. Colonel Hanson stretched his twisted ankle out farther on the camping stool, while Carole sat on the ground beside the fire and stared into the dancing orange flames. It had been a great weekend, she decided. Even if a lot of stuff had gone wrong, she and her dad had done some really fun things together. She was just about to thank him for the trip when she heard a noise at the edge of the forest.

"Did you hear something?" she asked her father.

"Yeah." Colonel Hanson twisted in seat. "It came from over there."

Carole looked over her shoulder and peered into the woods. Shadows seemed to be moving through the trees. Could it be Rambler on another nighttime visit? She squinted hard into the growing darkness. Her breath caught in her chest. Not Rambler, but Rambler's owners, the Loftins, stepped out of the forest.

"Hello," Mrs. Loftin called, her mouth barely stretching in a smile. "We thought we'd come say hello."

"Hello," Colonel Hanson's voice boomed through the clearing. "Come join us at the campfire."

"Hi." Carole quickly remembered her manners. She got up and unfolded two chairs for the Loftins. "Please come meet my father."

The Loftins walked over to the fire and shook hands with Colonel Hanson, then sat down in the chairs and seemed not to know what to do next.

"Uh, Dad and I were just finishing dinner," Carole said, "and we were about to toast some marshmallows for dessert. Would you join us?"

"Fine," said Mr. Loftin.

Carole ran to cut some more green sticks for the marshmallows. She wondered, as she searched among the bushes, if she should tell the Loftins about Rambler and their nighttime adventures. They were so strange they might get angry at both her and the horse. Maybe she should wait and see what turn the conversation took.

"My daughter tells me you're camping with horses." Colonel Hanson leaned forward in his chair.

"Yes. We have two Appaloosas that we camp with almost every weekend," Mr. Loftin said. "We used to go to the family campgrounds, but there were so many children who wanted to ride the horses that finally we just decided it would be better to tent camp farther out in the wilderness." Mr. Loftin looked at Colonel Hanson and gave a little laugh. "I couldn't allow strange children to ride my horses. Who knows what they would do to them?"

Colonel Hanson winked at Carole as she threaded marshmallows onto four sticks.

"And we were running into too many other horses at the family camps," Mrs. Loftin added. "Our horses could have actually caught diseases from those other animals!"

Colonel Hanson frowned. "I don't know that much about horses, but aren't they supposed to have some kind of vaccination before they come into the national parks?"

"Yes, but you still never know what kind of strange horse owners you might run into," Mr. Loftin replied with a frown.

Carole put the marshmallows over the fire. *Thank heavens I didn't mention Rambler,* she thought. *These people would probably sue me for horsenapping!*

"Say, you look like you're having some problems with your ankle." Mr. Loftin peered curiously at Colonel Hanson's elevated foot.

"I sprained it last night in the storm," he explained. "My daughter and I got stuck on top of Mount Stringfellow. We had quite a time getting down."

"What on earth were you doing up there in dark?" Mrs. Loftin asked with a frown.

"Stargazing," Colonel Hanson explained.

Mr. Loftin pushed his baseball cap back on his head. "How are you going to get back to your car? It's a long, steep trail down the mountain."

126

"Well, I'm not sure," Colonel Hanson said. "Carole and I haven't discussed it."

Carole gave the Loftins two green sticks loaded with marshmallows for them to toast, but before they began to cook them, Mr. Loftin shot a look at his wife.

"You know, I don't usually volunteer for rescue missions, but I could let you ride one of our horses down the trail," he said gruffly.

"But it would have to be in full daylight," added Mrs. Loftin. "And of course one of us would have to lead you. We couldn't possibly let a non-rider hold the reins himself."

"Yes. Our horses aren't used to anybody but us," said Mr. Loftin. "I hate to think what they might do. Horses don't like unfamiliar places or unfamiliar people."

Carole had to look at the ground to keep from laughing. These people had no idea how much their horse Rambler loved unfamiliar people and places. In fact, he had sneaked out of his paddock every night to find them!

Colonel Hanson smiled. "Well, that's a wonderful offer. I'd like to take you up on it, if you're sure I wouldn't upset your horse too much."

"Oh, don't worry." Mr. Loftin finished eating his marshmallows and stood up. "We'll be right here to make sure everything goes all right."

"What time shall we come back?" Mrs. Loftin stood up beside her husband. "It does need to be full daylight."

"How about ten o'clock?" Colonel Hanson suggested.

"Ten o'clock it is." Mr. Loftin nodded to Carole and her father as he and his wife stepped away from the campfire. "See you then. And thanks for the marshmallows. They were tasty."

"Bye," Carole said as the Loftins disappeared down the trail. She turned to her father and began to laugh.

"Can you believe how strange they are?" she asked.

"They're nice to help out, but they do seem a little overprotective." Colonel Hanson laughed too. "I think what you said last night was absolutely right— what the Loftins don't know about our Rambler won't hurt them."

"Well, they'll never hear about it from me or you." Carole laughed. "And Rambler will never tell!"

12

"I WONDER WHEN Carole will get back?" Stevie relaxed against one of the hay bales at the entrance of Pine Hollow. It was the first time since late Friday afternoon that she and Lisa had a chance to sit down for longer than five minutes.

"Soon, I hope," said Lisa. "I can't wait to show her Starlight. He just glows in his stall."

"We did do a good job with him, didn't we?" Stevie grinned. "He's one lucky horse."

"He is, but so are Danny and Patch and practically every other horse in the stable. We did a great job with them, too," added Lisa.

"That's right." A car pulled up in the driveway. Stevie leaped to her feet. "Here comes Max!" she cried. "We'd better get ready for inspection."

Lisa and Stevie stood together proudly as Max, his wife, Deborah, and Mrs. Reg got out of the car.

"Hi, girls!" Deborah called as she went to take Maxi, their daughter, out of her car seat. "How's it going?"

"Great," replied Stevie. "Did you guys have a good trip?"

"Wonderful." Mrs. Reg walked over and peered at Stevie and Lisa closely. "You two look a little tired."

"Well, we may have missed a couple of hours of our beauty sleep," admitted Lisa. "But nothing beyond that."

Max came up and stood beside his mother. "Okay. Are you two ready for inspection?"

Stevie and Lisa grinned and nodded.

"Then let's go."

Mrs. Reg and Deborah took Maxi to the house while Max slowly walked through the stable, checking every horse and stall. Stevie and Lisa followed in breathless silence. When Max got to the turn in the U-shaped structure, he turned and walked toward the foaling stall.

"There was a loose shutter in that stall," reported Stevie. "We closed it one night during a storm, and the next day we repaired it with a hammer and nails."

"Hmmmmm." Max looked at the shutter and nodded.

"And the lightbulb up there was burned out." Lisa

130

pointed to a fixture ten feet above their heads. "We got the long ladder and changed it."

"Hmmmmmm," Max said again.

He walked to the end of the aisle and turned back toward the front of the stable. Stevie and Lisa again followed as he checked every stall. They passed Prancer, who was standing against the back wall, a sad look on her face. Max stopped immediately.

"Why does Prancer look so down in the dumps?" he asked, lifting one eyebrow.

"I—I don't know," said Lisa. "We took care of her just like the other horses."

"Hmmmmmm," Max said a third time.

They continued, eventually coming to Starlight's and Belle's stalls.

"Wow," Max said when he saw Starlight in his stall. His coat looked as soft as velvet and his hooves shone as if he were going to a show. "Nice job on Starlight, but what's this on Belle?"

Max slipped into Belle's stall and ran his hands over her withers. His experienced fingers stopped at the small swelling Stevie's CD case had made.

"Uh, we had a slight accident," Stevie confessed. "I knocked one of my CD cases down through a hole in the hayloft. It hit Belle on the shoulder. I've been putting liniment on it."

"But we fixed the hole," Lisa added. "The same day we fixed the shutter."

"What about this water in the bottom of her stall?" Max frowned.

"Uh, I guess we forgot," Stevie said, suddenly embarrassed. "We just got so busy taking care of everybody else."

Max looked at them sternly. "I'm really impressed by what you two have done. Danny looks well rested, Starlight looks fabulous, everybody else seems to be in good shape, and the maintenance work around the barn is great. I have just one question."

"What?" Stevie and Lisa asked together.

"Why didn't you take care of your own horses as well? Prancer looks like she's lost her last friend, and Belle's standing in water with a good-sized bruise on her withers."

Lisa and Stevie look at each other, their mouths agape. They had no answer. Why hadn't they taken the best care of the horses they loved most? Suddenly all the other work they'd done seemed foolish.

"I don't know, Max," Lisa said. "I guess we just got so caught up in taking care of everything else, we put our own horses last."

"That's right," agreed Stevie. "I always felt like I could take care of Belle later."

Max sighed. "Well, I'm afraid you're going to have to take care of her now. Prancer, too. They need the same treatment Danny had last week. No riding, put

132

them out in the paddock with each other, and longe them every day."

"Do you think that will help?" Stevie was beginning to get scared. What if something really bad was wrong with Belle and she had ignored it?

"Yes, I'm sure they'll both be fine." Max smiled. "You guys just took too much care of the other horses and not enough care of your own."

"I guess the luckiest horse is the one who gets the care they need, not the extra things they really don't need," Lisa said, remembering the three groomings Starlight had endured each day.

"Right," said Max. "Now, go get busy. You've got horses to put out to paddock!"

"Okay." Stevie hurried over to Belle's stall while Lisa ran down to Prancer's. "And thanks, Max."

"Thank you, Stevie and Lisa. Other than these two things, you guys have done a great job!"

"OKAY." COLONEL HANSON adjusted the collapsible paddle under his arm and smiled at Carole. "Here goes nothing."

He took one step, then hopped on his good leg, then took another step. He grasped the paddle at a different angle and tried again. Step, hop, then step. Finally he turned and looked at Carole again.

"I'm sorry, honey. My ankle feels better, but I still

133

really can't put any weight on it." He sighed. "I'm afraid I'm not going to be much help in packing up this campsite."

"Oh, that's okay, Dad." Carole looked at all the stuff they'd dragged up there and forced herself to smile. "It'll just take a little longer."

"I can sit here and pack up the kitchen gear and the tent, though." Her father hopped over to the collapsible table and sat down. "That should help a little."

"Too bad the Loftins didn't volunteer their second horse to be a packhorse," Carole said wistfully, thinking of how many trips down and up the mountain she was going to have to make.

"I know," agreed Colonel Hanson. "But as nuts as they are about their horses, I guess we should consider ourselves honored that they offered to help at all."

"I suppose you're right." Carole began to make a pile of all the gear she thought she could carry down on her first trip. They were going to have to hurry if they were going to be all packed up by the time the Loftins arrived at ten.

She carried down all the chairs but one, the refrigerator, and the solar lamp on the first trip. By the time she returned for the second trip, her father had the tent down and all their bedding ready to go. When she returned for the final trip, the kitchen items were

134

packed and her father was standing on his canoe-paddle crutch, frowning.

"What's the matter, Dad?" she asked, wiping the sweat from her forehead. Even though the morning was cool, lugging stuff down a hill was hot work.

"I was just thinking about all this crazy stuff," Colonel Hanson said. "Here I am, a colonel in the Marine Corps, and I can't even help my daughter carry a down sleeping bag."

"Oh, Dad, don't feel bad. Accidents can happen to anybody. Even Marines."

"Yes, but just look at all this stuff. If I hadn't been so impressed with all Colonel Cheatham's gear, you could have been finished in just one trip!"

Carole flopped down on the ground. "Well, look at it this way. If we hadn't had all that stuff, we wouldn't have had the collapsible paddle for you to use right now." She grinned up at him. "I might have had to carve you a crutch out of green forsythia wood."

"I don't think there's any green wood left in this part of the forest," Colonel Hanson said, chuckling. "I think it's all been clear-cut for hot dog skewers!"

Carole laughed. She had enjoyed lots of her father's fancy equipment, but she'd enjoyed her own, simpler stuff, too. "Maybe the key is to take a few neat new things mixed in with our old standbys," she said.

"Right," said Colonel Hanson. "The Greeks had a word for that."

135

"Oh?" Carole looked up. "What?"

"Moderation."

Carole laughed. "Well, I guess I'd better moderate another load down to the car before the Loftins show up."

"I wish I could help you, honey."

"I know, Dad." Carole rose to her feet and grabbed the last three boxes. "Back in a flash."

By the time she returned from her final trip to the car, the Loftins were arriving with Rambler. The happy little horse now sported a full Western saddle, complete with saddlebags and two water canteens.

"This is Cisco," Mrs. Loftin said proudly. "He's an Appaloosa. It's a Western breed."

Developed by the Nez Percé Indians, Carole almost added, but stopped herself just in time. Instead she just smiled at her old friend Rambler. Though his real name was Cisco, he would always be Rambler to her. He tossed his head up and down as if to say hello.

Colonel Hanson gave Carole a quick wink, then tried to look afraid. "Gosh, he won't bite, will he?"

"Well, he might nip you if you feed him a carrot the wrong way," Mrs. Loftin said.

"Come on over here and let's get you up in the saddle," Mr. Loftin called. "You should always mount a horse from the left side." He looked at his wife. "Ethel, you be sure to hold him tight."

Mrs. Loftin grabbed the reins while Mr. Loftin helped Colonel Hanson mount the horse. Rambler stood calmly while the new, strange rider settled himself in the saddle.

"Now what?" asked Colonel Hanson, still playing dumb.

"Well, I'll take one side of the bridle and Ethel will take the other, and we'll get you down to your car. But don't kick him or try to make him go any faster!"

"Oh, no," said Colonel Hanson. "I certainly wouldn't want to do that."

Slowly the Loftins led Rambler and Colonel Hanson down and up the mountain trail. Carole followed, her father's canoe-paddle crutch and collapsible chair slung over her shoulder. It was funny to watch their parade from behind. There was her father, sitting tall in the saddle, and Rambler walking calmly, and then the Loftins on either side of the bridle, arguing over which side of the trail was safer. Carole shook her head. No wonder Rambler liked to ramble at night. It was probably the only way he got any fun at all!

Finally they clopped into the parking lot.

"That your station wagon?" Mr. Loftin asked.

Colonel Hanson nodded.

They led Rambler right to the driver's seat. Mrs. Loftin clutched Rambler's reins while Mr. Loftin again helped Colonel Hanson off the horse.

"Thank you so much," Carole's father said with a smile. "It was most kind of you to help us out."

"Oh, think nothing of it. We're glad to help, particularly if it lets us show off our horses." Mrs. Loftin gave Rambler a pat on the neck.

"Yeah." Mr. Loftin smiled for the first time since Carole had seen him. "We love our Cisco and Pancho a lot, and we take extra-special care of them." He rubbed Rambler behind his ears. "We figure they're pretty lucky horses to have owners like us!"

The Loftins backed Rambler up so that Colonel Hanson could scoot into the car. Carole gave the horse a final pat good-bye and got into the passenger seat. Colonel Hanson started the car, and with a wave to Rambler and the Loftins, they rolled out of the parking lot.

"Well, you just never know what kind of people you might run into in the woods," Colonel Hanson said with a laugh.

"I'll say," agreed Carole.

Still laughing softly, her father pulled onto the highway that led back to Willow Creek.

"How does your ankle feel when you drive?" Carole asked worriedly.

"Oh, it's a little tender, but I can certainly get us home." He reached into the glove compartment and fished out the cell phone. "Why don't you give Colonel Cheatham a call and tell him our situation? He and his sons can meet us at the house and help us unload all this gear."

"Okay." Carole smiled and punched in the number, grateful to be heading home.

"CAROLE!" STEVIE CRIED as she rounded the turn in the barn. "You're back!"

"Hi, Stevie! Hi, Lisa!" Carole turned away from Starlight as Stevie and Lisa ran toward her. They embraced in a three-way hug, happy to see one another after the long weekend.

"How did you guys do?" Carole asked. "Starlight looks terrific!"

"We said we'd take good care of him for you," Stevie said proudly. "And we are women of our words."

"How was your campout?" asked Lisa.

"Unbelievable." Carole rolled her eyes. "We had all this high-tech equipment and this mushroom-shaped tent and we got caught in a thunderstorm and my dad sprained his ankle and I almost got struck by lightning and—"

"What?" cried Stevie and Lisa, their eyes wide. "Struck by lightning?"

"Yeah," answered Carole. "And then—"

"Wait," said Lisa. "Why don't we go somewhere and sit down so you can tell us all about this slowly?"

"Okay," Carole said with a broad smile.

They got sodas from the refrigerator and walked to their favorite picnic place, the hill overlooking the paddocks. While Belle and Prancer frolicked in the field below, Carole told her friends all about fishing and stargazing and cooking on the solar stove.

"So your dad's all right now?" Stevie asked as Carole finished up her story.

"Yes. I helped him into the emergency room after Colonel Cheatham helped us unpack the car. He's got a bad sprain, but the intern said what I did had been exactly right. He even admired the way I wrapped Starlight's leg wrap on my dad's foot!"

Lisa giggled. "Did you tell him it was a horse bandage?"

"I had to," Carole laughed. "It was about a thousand feet too long to be a human bandage." She took a sip of soda and stretched out in the soft green grass. "So tell me about your weekend."

Stevie and Lisa looked at each other, then both began to tell Carole about how busy they'd been and about the CDs falling on Belle and Patch's nervousness at the thunderstorm and how Starlight hated Stevie's music so they'd put a babushka on his head, and that there had been a noise they'd thought was a ghost. When they finished talking, they were out of breath.

"Gosh," said Carole. "It sounds like you guys had a wild weekend, too."

"I don't think we sat down five minutes the whole time," Lisa replied. "But we learned an awful lot."

"Yeah," agreed Stevie. "Like sometimes the luckiest horse is the one that gets what they need, instead of a lot of extra stuff they don't need."

"That kind of sounds like our camping equipment," said Carole. "We had a lot of neat stuff, but we never even used most of it, and then I wound up having to carry all of it down to the car by myself. If those Loftin people had volunteered their other horse, I would have been here hours ago!"

"Huh?" Stevie and Lisa frowned. "What Loftin people?"

"Oh, didn't I tell you that?" said Carole. "The first night there I heard a whinny, and I followed it to a camp-site where this really unfriendly couple had two sweet Appaloosas corralled. That night, after we went to bed, one of them broke out of their paddock and came visiting! I took him back, but he came back the next night, too, right after the thunderstorm. I rode him up the mountain and he carried my father back to the camp."

"Wow!" exclaimed Lisa. "What a wonderful horse!"

"He was wonderful," Carole said. "I named him Rambler because of all his late-night rambles. But his owners were real jerks. They thought he was such a lucky horse to be owned by people like them, but he escaped twice from their camp and they didn't even know it! Even in a gigantic thunderstorm!" Carole sighed. "Poor guy. That doesn't sound like a lucky horse to me."

"Sure he was," Lisa said. "He was lucky enough to stumble on you that first night."

Carole frowned. "But I was the lucky one when he showed up the second night and carried my dad back to safety."

"That wasn't luck," Stevie said with a grin. "That was just plain old horse sense. The reason he came back to you was because you had taken such good care of him in the first place."

"Oh, Stevie," Carole laughed. She looked down at the horses playing, then turned and smiled at her friends. "I think we're all lucky. Let's go to TD's and celebrate!"

"The absolute final end of summer vacation?" Stevie asked.

"No," answered Carole. "The first faint beginnings of what I know is going to be a terrific school year!"

ABOUT THE AUTHOR

BONNIE BRYANT is the author of more than a hundred books about horses, including The Saddle Club series, Saddle Club Super Editions, the Pony Tails series, and Pine Hollow, which follows the Saddle Club girls into their teens. She has also written novels and movie novelizations under her married name, B. B. Hiller.

Ms. Bryant began writing The Saddle Club in 1986. Although she had done some riding before that, she intensified her studies then and found herself learning right along with her characters Stevie, Carole, and Lisa. She claims that they are all much better riders than she is.

Ms. Bryant was born and raised in New York City. She still lives there, in Greenwich Village, with her two sons.

Don't miss the next exciting
Saddle Club adventure . . .

DRIVING TEAM
The Saddle Club #90

The Saddle Club is gearing up to learn all about driving—not cars, horses. Carole Hanson and Lisa Atwood have to do an oral report on the use of driving teams throughout history. The only problem is that they have too much information! Somehow they have to rein in their enthusiasm, or their ten-minute talk could take a lifetime. Meanwhile, Stevie Lake is facing her worst nightmare. Her riding instructor wants Stevie to work with Veronica DiAngelo on a special driving team project: teaching their horses to work as a team. It's a great idea, but how are the horses going to work together if their owners can't? It'll take more than teamwork to get through this project—it'll take a miracle!

MEET
the SADDLE CLUB

Horse lover CAROLE...
Practical joker STEVIE...
Straight-A LISA...

THE SADDLE CLUB
SUPER EDITIONS

THE SADDLE CLUB
SPECIAL EDITIONS